Baird was an undercover agent for the North, and a rumored lunatic scheme for the South to take over Colorado provided cover of a sort . . . So he went in alone, under orders from Governor Gilpin, to find the originator of the scheme, his real and vital objective having nothing whatever to do with running down a hothead named Madison.

The way it was though, nobody could quite figure out whose side Baird was on. So it took quite a while, after he was "captured" by a Northern Army patrol, for him to convince them of his cover story.

By that time, a couple of other elements had entered the game . . .

Also by E. E. Halleran
Published by Ballantine Books:

SHADOW OF THE BIG HORN

DEVIL'S CANYON

SPANISH RIDGE

CIMARRON THUNDER

E. E. Halleran

BALLANTINE BOOKS • NEW YORK

ISBN 0-345-29492-0

Manufactured in the United States of America

First Edition: August 1970
Third Printing: July 1981

First Canadian Printing: August 1970
Second Canadian Printing: July 1981

CIMARRON THUNDER

Chapter 1

Baird knew that he had no choice but to follow the sign. The three riders ahead of him might well be enemies but they seemed to know where they were going. And that was more than he could say for himself. Twenty miles out of Bent's Fort he had decided that it had been a mistake to try for a direct approach to the Cimarron Cutoff but by that time it was too late to turn back. Time was pressing. He was already beginning to reckon it in hours instead of days.

He rode cautiously across the forbidding, barren land, the long fingers of one brown hand never far from the butt of the fine new Colt revolver he had bought in Denver. This stretch of wilderness between the two branches of the Santa Fe Trail had long been hideout country for renegades of two nations as well as for raiding bands of Comanches, Apaches and Utes. Two years of vicious war between North and South had sent deserters from both armies into the badlands. Baird didn't intend to let himself grow careless. Something pretty nasty seemed to be brewing down here below the Arkansas.

At the crossing of what he guessed was Two Butte Creek he had noticed that the three men ahead of him had scouted with great care. That was when he definitely marked the party as being three riders with one led horse. The group he hoped to locate would count eight men and four pack horses but he didn't waste time regretting that he had not cut the trail of the larger party. The Colorado scouts he needed to find should be on the Cimarron already. His best bet was to follow the trio ahead and hope that they would lead him through the wilderness of rock, sand and cactus to the Cimarron Trail. After that he would have to find some way of making contact with the right party.

It became clear that the men ahead were becoming increasingly cautious. After that well-scouted crossing of the dry creek they moved swiftly enough but always taking pains to avoid the more open stretches. It had not been easy to accomplish that purpose, Baird realized. He knew that he could not have taken the time to search out dry arroyos and ledges which these men seemed to use so well. Only someone who knew the country could have done it. As the last foothills of the Sangre de Cristos fell behind, the creeks died or disappeared into the sand. Setting a straight course for the Dry Cutoff was a real problem for anyone who didn't want to attract attention. He could count himself lucky that he had stumbled on the trail of someone who could do it.

He made a dry camp that night, lighting no fire and eating hard rations from his saddlebags. The big chestnut had to get along on the lifeless clumps of grass which grew between patches of dwarf cactus. The water was almost gone even though he had taken William Bent's advice about carrying a second canteen. He shrugged off the desire to be rid of the gritty dust and went to sleep as dirty and bewhiskered as he had ridden. The important thing was to get some of the kinks out of his long legs and some of the aches out of his back. It was physically humiliating to realize that he ached in so many places. The easy life of the past year had let him get soft. Now he had to pay the price.

More than that, he had to harden himself for what he knew would lie ahead.

In the first gray of dawn he was moving again, following the tracks as they swung in a wide arc to avoid a patch of flat desert. This was the Cimarron wasteland they had told him about. The Great American Desert, early travelers had called it. No more willows, wild plum or cherry along the creeks. No more creeks. Just deep, rock-filled gullies which would be raging torrents in the rainy season. Practically none of the tributaries of the Red or the Cimarron or the Arkansas carried water this late in the summer. The land was dry, hot, dull, ugly—and dangerous.

He calculated that he should reach the Cimarron Cutoff by late afternoon. That would give him time to dodge the men who had led him across the wasteland, perhaps even to make contact with the Colorado patrol before the messenger from Fort Union could arrive. There would probably be more than enough time. According to what they had told him in Denver and at Bent's Fort, travel to the Cutoff was likely to be slow. Daily sandstorms delayed wagons constantly.

At the country flattened out, he had to admire the cleverness of the men he followed. They were taking full advantage of every break in the terrain, always keeping themselves under the best available cover but still making good progress toward the Cimarron. In one arid stretch they even found a water hole. Baird gagged at the tepid, stagnant water but the big chestnut drank thirstily. Finding the tracks of these pacemakers was beginning to look more and more like a real piece of luck.

He became pretty curious about the trio. Deserters or outlaws? According to all accounts there were plenty of both passing through the area. They didn't live here. Nobody lived here. Outlaws simply used the wilderness for temporary shelter, moving out to raid government trains or isolated settlers. Perhaps these forays by desperate men were the real facts behind the wild rumors.

Baird hoped it would be that way. It would make his own job a little simpler even if it didn't lessen the danger.

Presently he began to know something about the men ahead. They operated on a pattern. In every danger spot two of them dismounted to wait while the third rider moved ahead to scout. Both of the men who waited were big, at least in their feet. They wore low-heeled boots of some sort, either miner's boots or brogans. The scout was barefooted. For a while Baird wondered whether the man might be an Indian but then he found a place where the trio had rested. The barefooted man had sprawled full length on loose sand, leaving the distinct imprint of a holster and gun belt. Indians were notoriously inclined to avoid handguns so it seemed likely that the scout was a New Mexican.

That gave Baird something to think about. William Bent had told him something of the Colorado patrol he was hoping to locate and Baird knew some regret that he had not listened more carefully. He remembered Bent saying that the leader was a Sergeant Jeremiah Flood, a hulking, short-legged man with a flowing mustache. There had also been mention of a New Englander named Warner. Bent had joked about the Yankee, calling him a gabby Vermonter. There had also been a reference to a young New Mexican referred to only as Luis. Since the First Colorado had been recruited largely from hardrock miners, it seemed quite possible that the boots were a good sign. Also the barefoot tracks. Maybe the men hurrying along ahead of him were three members of the force he hoped could help him.

The blistering sun was hot on his wet back, throwing a long shadow ahead, when he began to work into ridge country which seemed more like what he had seen along the Purgatory. He followed the tracks through a dry canyon and suddenly spotted a motionless horseman on the crest of a ridge which seemed to block the eastern end of the canyon. The man was perhaps a third of a mile ahead but in the slanting rays of the sun it was apparent that he was big. He was simply sitting his horse as though not interested in going anywhere or doing anything. There was nothing to indicate that he had any inkling of Baird's approach. He didn't turn his head to look into the west, possibly because the lowering sun made it impossible for him to see anything in that direction.

Baird hunched a little lower in his saddle, uneasily conscious of his own considerable size as he let the horse ease off to the right where a tumble of rocks offered some slight chance of concealment. Then he moved forward again, planning to dismount before reaching a spot where he might be too conspicuous. He had to find out why that fellow was sitting out there in the open so quietly.

There was a small patch of juniper among the rocks on one canyon wall so he moved up behind it, so intent on that curiously immobile figure ahead of him that he was caught completely by surprise when a harsh nasal voice ordered, "Git them hands up real high, mister! Quick now! I git powerful uneasy when folks fret me!"

A battered black hat rising from behind a boulder indicated the speaker's position, but at the same instant a second man broke from cover on the opposite side and trotted toward Baird, a big-bore carbine aimed at the prisoner. He was barefooted and wore a gun belt with a huge dragoon pistol sticking out of a homemade holster.

Baird knew a completely ridiculous sense of triumph when he noted the swarthy, youthful features under the big straw sombrero. At least he had guessed right about the barefooted scout being Mexican rather than Indian. Which was still mighty small satisfaction for a man who had let himself get trapped so easily.

Nonetheless the thought helped him to keep his voice calm. "No need to wave the artillery, gents. I'm not hostile. Just lost. It seemed like a good idea to follow the tracks of somebody who seemed to know where they were going. I wasn't . . ."

"Git down offa that hoss!" the nasal voice ordered. "Talk later. Luis, work around behind the bastard and git his guns. Careful now; he's a big 'un. Git the six-gun fust. Use it on him if he gits tricky." The speaker had come out into the open now, holding a cocked infantry musket ready for firing. Baird could see a tangle of gray whiskers half hidden by the musket, and the suggestion of a lean, bony face somewhere behind the whiskers. The man was as tall as Baird but not nearly so heavy. He was wearing bib overalls that were much too big for him, making his legs look somehow all the skinnier when the overalls flapped around them. Equally lean arms stuck out of the rolled-up sleeves of a faded army shirt. Corporal's chevrons appeared just above the roll of the sleeves. Which meant absolutely nothing, Baird knew. The combination of wholesale desertions and frequent raids on army supply trains had outfitted most of the outlaws in the territory with army gear.

Still, this man spoke with a real New England twang. And he had called his companion Luis. That added up hopefully. Baird tried to recall whether William Bent had said anything about the Vermonter being a corporal. Maybe it wasn't so pleasant a meeting after all. Perhaps these men had deserted from Flood's scout patrol. In that event they might be more dangerous enemies than casual outlaws, particularly if they had murdered the sergeant before deserting. Such things had happened many times in this wilderness.

"Bring yer hoss!" the graybeard ordered, a wave of the musket indicating that the command was aimed at Baird. "Luis, stick right on his tail. Keep yer gun cocked. Time enough fer talk when we git outa this damned open spot."

Baird followed the orders meekly enough. There was no point in doing anything else and he needed time to figure things out. As yet he could not be sure whether he had been lucky or the exact opposite.

They started to climb the gravel slope toward the spot where the big man still sat his horse. Almost at once Baird could see two saddle ponies and a pack horse concealed behind a rocky outcrop. It was now quite clear that the trio had spotted him on their back trail and had laid a rather neat trap. The big man had deliberately drawn attention to himself while the others waited for their game to move into range for capture.

It was the hulking decoy who broke the silence. "How about it, Ethan?" he asked. "Do ye figger it's him?" He was even bigger than Baird but a good ten years younger, only a trace of yellow fuzz showing on the square chin but with more than a fair share of yellow hair bushing out under the shapeless brown hat. What caught Baird's attention most were the penetrating blue eyes. They were angry eyes, somehow out of place in those inscrutable features. The big youth might look slightly stupid but Baird decided not to bet on it.

"We're fixin' to find out jest as soon as we know we ain't gonna have no company," the graybeard told him. "Any sign o' snoopers up there?" He jerked a gnarled thumb toward the top of the ridge as he spoke.

"Nothin' movin'. I reckon them polecats won't be climbin' the ridge jest to look at scenery—and they sure as hell don't know we're near 'em."

"We'll find out fer sure. Luis, take a look."

The dark-faced youth swung wide to hand over the Sharps carbine he had taken from Baird's saddle scabbard, keeping the Colt revolver in the waistband of his faded denim pants. Then he swung into the saddle of one of the hidden ponies and began a brisk but cautious climb, his angle taking him well away from what would have been the direct line to the top.

Baird could now understand how they had happened to spot him on their back trail. Some enemy had been seen beyond this next ridge and the retreating trio had been startled to find another possible enemy behind them.

Before he could think much about it, the older man waved a gun at him and snapped, "Set down there on the ground, Captain Madison! Ye won't be goin' no-where fer quite a spell so ye might as well ease yer carcass. Them bastard friends o' your'n on the far side o' the ridge don't even know ye're in trouble—so don't depend on 'em."

He was staring hard as he snapped out the final phrases. Baird knew what it meant. The use of the name had been an attempt to surprise the prisoner into some sort of reaction, perhaps an admission that he was the man named.

"Nice try, Corporal," Baird said with a grin which was not too hard to put on. The move had told him something. These men were definitely on the right side. "If I'd been Madison I kinda think you'd have sur-prised me into admitting it. It happens that I'm not Madison."

The old man was still studying him narrowly. "Any way o' provin' ye ain't?"

"I think so. First, let me tell you that I'm Tom Baird. I'm down here as a sort of special agent of Governor Gilpin of Colorado. Up Denver way they're a mite worried over this man Madison. They want to know if he's hanging out along the Cimarron and why. I'm supposed to find out."

The big fellow on the horse snorted in disbelief. "They tole us the Reb was a smooth article, Ethan. Don't swaller none o' that fancy gab."

"I don't swaller easy," Ethan retorted. "Git on with yer tale, Mister Governor's Man. How was ye supposed to be findin' this Madison feller in country like this?"

"I was told that the First Colorado Cavalry had a scout patrol down here. They were on much the same job but none of them know Madison by sight. I do. I was to locate the patrol and pass along my orders to a Sergeant Flood."

"Yeah? Supposin' I was to tell ye I'm Flood?"

"Then you'd be lying. Flood's a stocky man, shorter than you and a lot wider. Also maybe a trifle younger —like twenty years or so."

"Don't git smart!"

"No offense meant. I think your name is Warner. William Bent told me about you. I didn't get that part of my information in Denver."

"Mebbe ye got it from that bastard Flood! Dirk, climb down and git around behind this varmint. We'll have to see what he's got in his pockets. Leave yer gun behind. Ain't no point in givin' him no chance to grab it. I'm keepin' him covered fer ye."

Baird grinned amiably at the older man. "I think I'm going to like you, Corporal Warner. You think real good and you do something about it."

He was still trying to see something other than suspicion in the old man's eyes when Dirk circled around to his rear. There was a crunch of heavy boots on the gravel and then it seemed as though somebody had tried to take his head off. A blow behind his right ear sent him sprawling to the ground. Through the haze of semiconsciousness he heard a hoarse chuckle and Dirk's happy, "That oughta hold him fer a spell, Ethan. If'n he don't talk up real pert, I kin give him another dose."

There was a moment of silence and then Dirk added —almost anxiously—"He won't be tryin' no tricks on us now, Ethan. We gotta learn him who's boss around here."

Chapter 2

Baird knew an uncomfortable feeling of sand in his mouth. He was dizzy from the blow but his mind reached out for a couple of rather odd ideas. He decided that the burly Dirk was in some awe of Warner. His tone had been definitely that of someone looking for approval.

He didn't get it. The twangy voice broke through Baird's private little fog to demand, "Now why'n hell did ye have to do that, Dirk? Don't ye ever git tired o' showin' off yer muscles? This feller kin be jest what he claims to be."

"We'll dam' soon find out," Dirk growled. He stooped to go through Baird's pockets, cursing when he found them empty.

Baird remained inert, letting his head clear. He felt pretty certain of his men now. He could even appreciate their caution in a country where treachery was commonplace. Still, he didn't let himself get carried away by thoughts of friendship. People who slugged Tom Baird from the rear had something coming to them.

He waited until Dirk rolled him over in order to probe at shirt pockets. Then he rolled swiftly, slamming a hard fist against the fuzzy chin so close to him. The blow had enough power to enable him to get his feet under him and throw a real punch when Dirk howled in for an angry attack. Dirk was strong but he was not a clever fighter. Baird landed his first punch and the blond youth went down. He didn't even grunt.

Baird froze then, half expecting a shot. Gradually he turned his head to stare at the musket which was aimed at his belt buckle. "You were right, Ethan. Dirk shows off his muscle too much. Now can we get down to business?"

Warner let his straggly whiskers pucker into a brief show of amusement. Then he snapped, "Hold it, Dirk! We had plenty o' that. Let's hear what he's got to say fer hisself. He said he had proof about who he is. We want to see it."

Dirk had clambered to his feet by this time, rubbing his jaw and aiming a crooked grin at Baird. "I kinda hope he's got it, Ethan. He hits hard. We better hope he's on our side." He didn't seem to hold any grudges.

Baird stooped to pick up the black campaign hat which had been knocked from his head by that first blow. "You looked in the wrong place, Dirk," he said quietly. "My orders from Governor Gilpin are under the sweatband of the hat. Who wants to look at 'em?"

"Drop the paper on the ground," Warner ordered. "Then back up. Git yer gun, Dirk. I'm goin' to be a mite busy studyin' out the kind o' words what goes into fancy papers. Keep him covered."

There was a silence while the Vermonter picked up the paper and squinted hard at it, his lips forming the words with apparent difficulty. Then he motioned for Dirk to lower his gun.

"Bein' as how I've seen that scrawl o' Bill Gilpin's before—when he wasn't sech a important galoot as he's got to be lately—I'd say ye're all right. Leastways, he thinks so." He stepped forward to hand back the paper. "Now mebbe ye'd better explain yerself a bit more." His tone suggested that he was almost convinced but not quite.

Baird made a careful business of folding the paper

and tucking it back into place beneath the sweatband of the hat. The delay gave him time to decide on how much he ought to tell these men. The success of his mission might well be dependent on their cooperation, yet he didn't want to say too much. The Colorado authorities had suggested the Madison story as one good way to cover his true business in the area. After his talk with William Bent he had worked out a few variations to match the conditions supposed to exist along the Cimarron. Now he decided to stick pretty much to the first version. It not only was true but it could be expanded later if he decided to trust the Colorado scouts all the way.

"Like I told you, my name is Tom Baird. I worked for the company that built the telegraph line along the old Overland Trail. Before that I was in the army. I resigned my commission to take the telegraph job. It happens that I knew a cadet at West Point named Joe Madison. Most folks believe that this is the same fellow known as Captain Madison out here. They know in Washington—and in Denver—that he tried hard to recruit Confederate volunteers along the Arkansas, probably to join Sibley when he came up from the Rio Grande. When Sibley had to retreat after the Apache Canyon fight, Madison disappeared. Now there are rumors that he's back again. My job is to find out about it."

"Won't be no trouble findin' plenty o' Madison talk," Warner told him. "Sure as hell there's trouble brewin'. Likely he's behind it."

"So far it's just talk. Nobody knows. Madison could be important. He recruited a lot of men for that army he had in training over in Mace's Hole. If he's back again, the government wants to know it."

"What the hell difference does it make?" Dirk broke in. "Somebody's stirrin' up trouble down this way. If'n it ain't Madison, it's somebody else jest as bad."

"Somebody in Washington thinks it's important," Baird explained patiently, knowing that this was the point where he had to get his possible allies thinking properly. "Nobody doubts that there's trouble building along the Cimarron. There's *always* trouble along the Cimarron. If it's the usual collection of outlaws, renegades, drunken Comanches and deserters causing the trouble, then it's up to local folks to take care of it. But if Madison's at the root of it, then there's a chance that the Confederacy is trying to use this area as a jumping-off place for some such invasion as the one Sibley tried. Have you men heard any mention of the Pecos Volunteers?"

"Yep," Warner said shortly. "That's what some folks called the crowd what was movin' up the Pecos to join Sibley—only he never got to a place where they could join him. Our fellers seen to that!"

Baird nodded. "Were you at Apache Canyon?"

"Yep."

"Good job. Is it possible that the name—Pecos Volunteers, I mean—has been meaning something else lately?"

"Not as I know."

"What about Cimarron Thunder? Have you heard anybody use that phrase?"

"Nope."

"Then I'll tell it to you as it was told to me. The Federal government has been getting a lot of hints about a possible attempt by Confederates to strike at Colorado. Possibly they have the same idea of separating the west coast from the rest of the country, the way Sibley did. Military headquarters thinks there may be a secret army gathering for the invasion. That army has been given the name Pecos Volunteers. Their plan of attack has a code name. Cimarron Thunder. Does it make any sense to you—with what you already know about matters down here?"

Warner shook his head. "I ain't had a hint about it. On the other hand, I ain't heard a thing to make me call it a pipe dream."

"So that's why I'm here," Baird went on. "If there's

big trouble working up—the kind of trouble a man like Joe Madison might be organizing—the government wants to make some moves. They'll send troops. If it's only a false alarm, set up to make 'em send the troops perhaps, then they want to know the truth. They can't afford to pull out any more men than necessary from the reserves Grant and Sherman and the others are going to need in Tennessee and along the Mississippi. Does that make sense?"

"Seems like. So they sent ye down here because ye'd know Madison if'n ye seen him. Right?"

"Right."

Dirk broke in with a jeer in his voice. "Ye mean ye're supposed to git close enough to the bastard to recognize him—and then git away to tell folks back east? How did the smart boys in Denver or wherever figger how ye'd manage it?"

Baird grinned crookedly. "Dirk, my friend, you should know that the smart boys at headquarters never figure out things like that. It's up to me. Either I work it out some way for myself or I don't get back. Simple, eh?"

"Ye're expectin' us to help ye?" Warner asked.

"I had hopes. You've got partly the same assignment, I believe. You're down here to find out what's brewing and whether Madison is back of it. You're even a mite nervous about him. When I showed up on your rear you thought I might be Madison. You . . ."

"We heard so much about Madison that we kinda expect to see him behind every rock!"

"So you're working on the same job as me. They told me in Denver that I might expect to get some help from a patrol commanded by Sergeant Flood."

"That goddam Flood!" Dirk exploded. "He won't be helpin' nobody if'n I once git him lined up in gunsights!"

Warner motioned him to silence. "Git on your hoss, Baird," he ordered hurriedly. "Luis is comin' back down the hill. We'll talk some more after we find out what's happenin' beyond the ridge."

All of them mounted then, Warner keeping Baird's carbine. It was clear that he wasn't ready to trust his prisoner entirely. And he had been pretty quick to stop Dirk talking about Flood. Something was wrong that Baird couldn't quite understand.

While they were moving to meet the New Mexican, the older man seemed to thaw. He even sounded good-natured as he asked, "How come ye told us all that yarn so fast, Baird? Seems like a man on a partickler errand fer the gov'ment oughta go slow with the talk. What makes ye think ye kin trust us?"

Baird shrugged as though it didn't seem important to him. "It seemed safe enough. You tried to trick me into admitting that I was Joe Madison. If you were mixed up with him you'd know better. He's not at all like me. If all you know about him is that he's an enemy—then you're on my side."

"Sounds reasonable."

Luis was just ahead and Warner made a show of turning his attention to the scout.

Luis made his report promptly. "They stay where we saw them. By the old trail. I do not know why they are there." His accent was slight, only the vowels hinting at Spanish background. "Still the same six men."

"Flood with 'em?"

"I cannot be sure." The swarthy youth seemed to speak with a certain precision, as though he had learned his English from a book rather than from the rough contacts of the border country. "There is much steeper grade at the bottom of the slope on this side. I cannot see the men on the near side without exposing myself to those beyond the trail."

"He's there, all right," Dirk growled. "I know that squatty bastard even at a distance. And I seen the hoss he stole from me!"

Warner waved him off. "We'll camp here tonight. Come mornin' we take a closer look. Mebbe we'll even shoot 'em up a bit." He glanced significantly at Luis and then motioned toward Baird. "This gent is mebbe all right. I ain't jest sure yet."

He changed his tone as he gave orders for setting up a camp that would serve the purpose and still not let the possible enemy know that they had neighbors. The four men simply moved into a little pocket between rock ledges, picketing the horses where fragments of dried grasses made a brave showing among some stunted junipers. There would be no fire. Hard rations and a sip of water for each. Water was the big problem for everybody in this arid waste.

The three Coloradans seemed to ignore Baird as they talked freely among themselves. They made no attempt to keep him from overhearing but at the same time they were careful to keep him away from themselves or their weapons. He learned that they had made their direct approach to the Cimarron Cutoff in an effort to catch up with Sergeant Flood but he couldn't quite make out what had happened to make them now regard their former commander as their enemy.

At any rate, they had approached the Cutoff trail just in time to find another party making camp beside it. Four of the six men in the other group were wearing bits of Federal uniforms but that meant nothing. Many enlisted men of southern background had deserted when their officers resigned and left to join the Confederate armies. Many of them had not gone south but had remained to join outlaws in raids on isolated settlements or on wagon trains. The confusion following Sibley's attempt to invade Colorado had added to the problem. No one knew how many desperadoes were moving about in the region between the Sangre de Cristos and the Indian territories south of the Arkansas. Most of them would be wearing bits of Federal uniform stolen from army supplies or brought along by deserters.

After a time the three scouts began to talk in lower tones and Baird knew they were talking about him.

Probably they were trying to decide how he should be treated during the night.

Presently Warner loafed across to where Baird was stretched out on the bare ground, his head aching a little from the blow Dirk had given him, the rest of him aching still worse from so many hours in the saddle. Warner wasted no time on preliminaries. "How well did ye know Jerry Flood?" he demanded.

"I didn't know him at all. I told you that."

"Ye knowed what he looked like."

"Sure. William Bent gave me the description. You men were at his post a week or so before I arrived. There were eight of you then."

"Does Bent know what you're doin' down here?"

"Yes. I had orders to tell him. Bent has proved himself loyal to the Union by keeping the Cheyennes clear of this Indian trouble that's supposed to be shaping up."

"Up to now he has," Warner grunted. "I dunno how long he can keep doin' it."

"Maybe all this rumor of Indian trouble is like the Captain Madison talk. Plenty of Rebs would like to stir up real trouble but I've got a hunch that the responsible officials aren't dealing with Indians. It'll serve their purpose well enough if they can scare the federal government into sending troops out here. Anything to relieve the pressure on Johnston or Lee or Hood will suit the South very well."

"Mebbe. But this Injun trouble ain't never gonna be easy. Likely enough the Comanches and Kiowas won't help Texans none but they've still got plenty o' young hotheads what don't care who they fight as long as they fight. The chiefs ain't stupid enough to mix up in a white man's war when they kin let white men kill each other—but they'll sure as hell take whatever advantage they git out of it. And they won't push real hard to keep the young hellions from bustin' loose."

Baird had the distinct feeling that Warner was really opening up, expressing his real worries and at the same time trying to see what kind of reaction he would get from a stranger. "Likely you're right. Do you think there are enough of these young Indian hoodlums to cause real trouble?"

"I'm damned sure of it! What's to stop 'em? The posts along the Arkansas ain't got men enough to defend their own quarters. They don't even try to send guards with wagon trains. Last month there was thirty-three men in Fort Larned and thirty-nine in Fort Lyon. Mebbe half of 'em could be called fightin' men. They couldn't hope to stop even small raids."

"At the moment our main worry is not Indians. Do you think that the men on the other side of the ridge are simply outlaws, or are they a part of this mysterious Rebel plot we've been talking about?"

"I ain't sure. All we know is that they're killers!" The words came out savagely but there was something else in the tone besides. It seemed to Baird that Warner was feeling his way through the talk, trying to make up his mind about something.

"You think Sergeant Flood is with them?" he asked quietly. If the Flood angle was what was troubling the Vermonter, maybe he could be prodded into talking about it.

"Flood's with 'em, all right! He's the worst murderer in the lot."

"Are you sure?"

"Damned sure." He hesitated before adding, "If'n I tell ye how I know, would ye be interested in j'inin' up with us to help wipe 'em out?"

"You were planning to attack six men? Only the three of you?"

"We could do it—but four would make it easier." His tone became a little more crisp but the words seemed to come out with an added caution. He was almost reciting as he went on, "With four of us we could attack from both sides. Two on one side, two on the other."

Baird stared hard into the gathering darkness, surprise making him silent for a moment. He felt sure that Warner had carefully worked up to that final bit of phrasing. It was not what he expected but he liked it. "Two and two," he said slowly, almost matching the Vermonter's tempo. "It's a mighty fine combination."

Warner made no reply in words. He simply edged across and stuck out a bony hand, giving Baird the secret grip, the fingers forming the two and two sign. Only then did he ask formally, "Where'd ye jine the Loyal League?"

Baird grinned thinly at the attention to ritual. "I didn't," he replied. "I joined the Union League."

Warner chuckled happily. "So we're both members of the National Loyal Union League. That oughta make things a mite easier. Now tell me how many lies ye've been feedin' me."

"None," Baird assured him. "I didn't suspect that you were a League member but I figured I'd be working with you. It seemed better to tell the truth. Now you'd better do the same thing. What the hell happened to Flood?"

Chapter 3

Warner still hesitated. Then he muttered, "Let's move over with the other boys. They don't belong to the League but they're to be trusted. We'd better let 'em know that we're workin' together all the way."

They made the move in silence. Then Warner growled, "Better listen to this, fellers. I tested out Mister Blair and he's on our side all right. He'll lend a hand. I'm goin' to tell him about Flood. Chime in if'n I got any part of it that needs patchin'."

Neither of the men replied but Baird knew that both had rolled over to listen. Warner went ahead slowly, picking his words as though trying to make sure that he was keeping the story completely clear. "Gittin' this scout party together wasn't easy. We had to use fellers from around Denver because there's too many Secesh down here along the Arkansas. No tellin' how many of 'em was mixed up in that Mace's Hole crowd so it wouldn't do to send 'em on a chore like this'n. Luis was the only good man on hand what knowed this Godforsaken country. When Jeremiah Flood asked to git into the party the folks at headquarters was plumb impressed. He claimed he'd been all through the Cimarron country. They put him in command."

"Instead of you?" Baird asked, his tone suggesting nothing.

"Yep. But don't think it bothered me none. I wasn't none too keen on ramroddin' this gang of hardheads. Flood was welcome to the command. We took the word of a couple o' Denver idiots what said he was a good man."

"Which he wasn't," Luis murmured from his shadow.

"He is a no-good sonofabitch!" Warner growled. "After we left Bent's Fort we moved around to talk with some o' them ranchers and farmers near there. It seemed smart enough. Them varmints is mostly Secesh and we kinda figgered Flood might pick up a hint about this here Captain Madison. We never suspected that he was workin' out a deal to sell us out.

"Along the Picketwire he ordered us to split up for searchin' two separate bits o' country. Us three was to move on up the canyon of the Picketwire—or Purgatory, as some calls it. The other four was to swing east and scout along the Two Butte Creek. Flood claimed he had to ride back to Fort Bent and pass along a report. We was to meet up again on Two Butte Creek."

"I can get ahead of you a little there," Baird commented. "I know that Flood didn't go back to Bent's Fort."

"Right. He headed east with a pack horse what belonged to Dirk—which makes him a hoss thief among other things. But let me tell it the way it happened to us. We was lucky. Luis slipped outa camp the fust night to visit a lady friend on a ranch near us."

"Cousin," Luis supplied drowsily.

"Cousin, hell! Luis has got more cousins between here and Santa Fe than a town dog's got fleas. He don't pay no heed to the he cousins, but the she ones sure git visited plenty! Anyhow, he got a earful from this one and was back in camp around midnight—which mostly he don't manage. The Mexes on that ranch had heard plenty and they told it all to Cousin

Luis. Flood had made a deal with a polecat named Barney Oakes. Flood was to git rid of us fellers and jine Oakes along the Cimarron fer somethin' or other. That part the Mexes didn't know about."

"And you think the story was all true?"

"We know damned well it was true! Luis knew where a gang of cutthroats was to ambush us and wipe us out next mornin'. He also knowed how to git to that spot without ridin' up the canyon. We got there fust." He paused significantly before adding, "I kinda reckon Oakes and Flood are gittin' a mite anxious to hear from them bastards."

"What happened to the other four from your squad?"

"We buried 'em. They got wiped out jest like we was supposed to be. That's when we headed fer the Cimarron."

"And you think these men across the ridge are the ambushers of the other part of your patrol?"

"Who else?"

Baird didn't argue the point. "One more thing," he said. "Then we'd better get some sleep. You'd better know that this Cimarron Thunder thing I mentioned isn't all rumor. A lot of reports have been trickling in to Washington. They get back here by telegraph. The story is that when Sibley came up the Rio Grande he was to be joined by a detachment coming up the Pecos."

"We covered that," Warner reminded him.

"Not entirely. When the Pecos force retreated to the Rio Grande after Sibley was turned back, they left a cache of arms and ammunition behind them. Nobody seems to know exactly where. This Cimarron Thunder scheme might be something to do with using those munitions for a new attack on Colorado or on the Arkansas forts."

"And ye're supposed to look into that? Along with the Madison bit?"

"That's right. Can we swap off a bit of help?"

"Ye've got a deal. Good night."

"Not yet. I'm not the only one trying to find out the truth. A Federal agent has been working around Fort Union on the same errand. He's supposed to be coming up the Dry Cutoff right now. I'm supposed to keep an eye out for him and help him get through to Fort Larned. Can I depend on you to lend a hand there if the trouble gets bad?"

"Still a deal," Warner grunted. "Good night again."

Baird woke to a chill dawn, stars as brilliant as though the time were December instead of late August. That was the way it was in this country, he knew. Broil by day and shiver by night. He heard someone moving on the gravel slope above him and instantly forgot his discomfort. As he scrambled to his feet, Warner's nasal tones came lazily.

"Don't fret yerself, Baird. It's jest Luis headin' fer the top o' the ridge. He wants to be ready fer a good look when daylight comes. When he reports, we'll make our move."

"What moves?"

"Dunno yit. Depends on what the other side is tryin' to do. I been thinkin'. When we seen 'em yestidday it looked like they was fixin' to wait there fer somebuddy. It ain't Flood; he's there already. Mebbe they know about this messenger comin' up the Cutoff Trail. Could be they're plannin' to grab him."

"More likely they're after wagons."

"Nope. Wagons ain't usin' this trail now. No water. I kinda figger that these outlaws was workin' Raton Pass but moved over here because Oakes or somebuddy had a job to do. Could be yer messenger."

"Then we'd better get ready."

"So gnaw on some hardtack. When Luis comes back we'll be all set."

No mention had been made of rank or command. Baird had not thought it necessary to state that he had been commissioned a captain when he went back into government service. For the present it seemed better to let Warner continue as official head of the little force. Pulling rank could come later if it seemed necessary.

He stood erect for a moment or two, noting with some satisfaction that a lot of the aches had left him. There was still a sore spot behind his ear but he didn't mind. Dirk was probably nursing a sore chin. He brushed some of the gravel out of his stubble of sandy whiskers and turned to his canteen. One had been left with his saddle since it was already empty. A few drops of the stale water was all that he wanted so he sat down to wait. Going hungry wouldn't be too bad. Better than chewing dry hardtack.

Luis came down from the crest as the other two were finishing their hardtack and bad water. Dawn had arrived.

"Still there," the New Mexican reported. "Six men along the old trail and one of them is certainly Flood. By the way they are pointing I think they plan to spread out on both sides of the trail. They have hidden their horses in a notch north of where they now are holding their powwow."

"Looks like a ambush, all right," Dirk growled.

"Of someone on the way up from Fort Union," Luis continued. "If the horses are north of the ambush spot, they will not be seen until it is too late for escape. Also, in case the victims prove too tough, the horses are in position for retreat to the north."

"Ye think things out real good, Luis," Warner approved. "Let's git movin'. We leave the hosses right where they're at. This has got to be done on foot. Luis, take Baird with ye. Make fer that strip o' rocks we seen yestidday. Try to work yer way down along the south side of it 'til ye're in good gunshot o' them varmints. If any of 'em is holed up in the rocks, don't git low enough to skeer 'em 'til we're ready. Understand?"

"How do we know when to attack?" Baird asked. "It had better be well timed. We're still outnumbered, remember."

"I'm figgerin' on that. Me and Dirk will flank 'em on the north where that gulley leads down to their horse hidin' place. When we're in a spot where we kin cut 'em off from their hosses, we open fire. Then ye let 'em have it."

"First slug to Flood," Dirk said grimly.

"That's yer own personal job," Warner agreed. "The rest of us pick the best targets we kin see. Cut the odds quick."

They separated without further talk, Baird glad enough that he had come to an agreement with the Colorado men. Attacking from the rear gave him a certain sense of revulsion, but he reminded himself that this was the way of guerrilla war. The men they proposed to shoot down were either guerrillas or plain murderers. There was no reason to have qualms about executing them.

He made no comment when his own weapons were restored to him. He had a strong feeling that Luis hated to give up the revolver, but neither of them commented. They simply headed up the slope at a long angle to the right. Meanwhile, Dirk and Warner seemed to be making an even longer sweep to the left. The morning was still and silent, the red of the sunrise having turned to more of a yellow glare which now outlined the ridge top in bold silhouette. It all looked peaceful enough in spite of its bareness. Somehow, it was hard to believe that cold-blooded murderers were on the far side of the slope—and that more murder was in the planning.

He didn't let himself worry over the fact that he would probably be doing some of the killing. That part had been a strong probability when he started on the job. This was just another military operation. It had to be done by somebody.

Presently Luis motioned for a halt. "The others have a longer circle to make," he murmured. "We wait. You will see that the trail runs through a gully beyond this ridge. You will not see much of the trail when we cross the top. There is a bulge in the ridge which hides the bottom. I think that the ambushers on this side will be below the bulge. We will not see them until we are almost to trail level—but any men waiting on the farther slope, beyond the trail, will see us. We must take care."

"I get the idea. Now tell me something else. I forgot to ask last night. Did your friends feel that Flood had made a deal with Oakes or was it the other way around?"

"They think Oakes has a plan to steal something very valuable. He wanted Flood to help him. It is likely that Flood had heard about it and was searching to find Oakes. Do you know of Oakes?"

"No. I've never been in this part of the country before."

"He is a bad one. My people fear him. Many men he has killed, not all of them in holdups. In the Ratons he is feared by many. My people think that he has a plan to steal much loot and wished Flood to help him."

"Any chance that this loot might be the arms I mentioned last night?"

Luis shook his head soberly. "It is not very likely. Oakes is not on the side of either the Union or the Confederacy. He is against everyone. If there is money at the cache—he would be interested. Guns—maybe."

"And where does Flood fit in? What do you know about him?"

"Not very much. I only know that he was enlisted in the company that mutinied when they were marching across Raton Pass on the way to stop Sibley's army. Flood joined the officers against the mutineers. Major Chivington promoted him to sergeant."

"Sounds pretty loyal."

"Not Flood. He is a bully. He hated the men who rode beside him. When he became sergeant he could bully them." The youth paused for a moment before adding with a crooked grin, "I think he made friends with them again when they reached Fort Union. He was very busy when the Colorado troops broke loose and plundered the fort's stores. I heard that he was selling stolen whiskey for a week or more. He sobered up in time to make a brave show of driving the drunks back into their proper places—so he kept his stripes."

"I begin to get the picture. Why did they send him on this mission?"

"He knows the Cimarron country. I am sure of that. I talked with him about it. I think perhaps Barney Oakes wanted him for that same reason. Oakes knows every nook and cranny in the Raton mountains but he does not know the Cimarron." He gestured upward. "I think we must move now. Ethan and Dirk have had time to make their circle."

Baird saw that he was headed toward a spot where the crest of the gravel ridge showed rough against the morning's glare. Rocks stuck up out of the sand in several places and Warner's orders began to make sense. They were to use these rocks for concealment unless the enemy had already occupied the area.

When Luis halted again, they were well hidden by a whole cluster of the brown crags. He motioned for Baird to crawl in beside him and the tall man sighted along a pointing finger. There was low ground immediately in front but the actual trail was still hidden. Perhaps two hundred yards away, where the ground sloped upward again, he could see two men squatting beside clumps of juniper. Apparently, they had selected their ambush positions, but had not yet bothered to conceal themselves.

"Three more on this side, I think," Luis whispered, the final word carrying a real trace of accent. "One man has gone south along the trail to act as scout."

Baird wondered whether the break in the youth's usual precise English was a sign of excitement. If so, it was the only sign. Luis seemed to be doing an ordinary job in an ordinary way.

"Now we go on down," he whispered. "Crawl always, from rock to rock. The light is full on us and those men beyond the trail will see any small movement."

Baird followed again. It wasn't exactly a comfortable business to crawl through gravel where the only vegetation seemed to be dwarf cactus. It was even more uncomfortable to realize that any careless move might bring a bullet. Still, it was the only possible way of preparing for the attack. This enemy could not be hit from the ridge top. Baird and his Colorado friends had to see their targets before they could hit them.

"One thing I didn't mention," Baird murmured when they paused for another observation. "When you're dealing with bandits, you don't take prisoners—but I'd kinda like to get one. Maybe we could make him do some talking."

Luis turned to give him a boyish grin. "Only if he is the last one. We are outnumbered. Please to remember that." Somehow the grin and the words didn't go together.

They could now see across the angle of the hump which had concealed the trail. Ruts showed faintly in stretches where blowing sand had not covered them. Not many wagons were using the Cutoff. More important than the trail, however, were the lounging men who could now be distinguished. Three were on the near side, as Luis had guessed, all within fair range. Like the pair on the opposite slope, they held positions near bits of cover but had not yet made any attempt to hide.

"Looks nasty," Baird whispered. "They're ready for a massacre, not a holdup."

"As they did with our men," Luis told him bitterly. "These are killers."

"Is your man Flood out there?"

"This side. Last one across. Dirk will be pleased to find it so."

"When do we hit them?"

Luis turned his head to stare quizzically. "Ethan did not tell you that part? Perhaps he feared you would not like it. We open fire when they make their attack. We catch them by surprise while their guns are empty. We are outnumbered. It is the only way."

"You don't need to explain—but I can't wait for them to kill the fellow I'm supposed to meet!"

"I do not give the orders," Luis said flatly. "I only tell you what Ethan wants. These men have murdered our friends. We do what we must." Then he added uneasily, "Perhaps your man will not be hit when they fire."

Chapter 4

There was no opportunity to argue the matter. Baird
heard the rapid clop of hoofbeats in the sand just as
brown fingers closed on his arm in warning. There was
a fleeting glimpse of a rider coming up from the south
but then the man was out of sight behind the rocks.
Baird had a sudden foolish notion that perhaps he was
permitting the government messenger to ride into a
trap, but then he recalled that the ambushers had sent
their sixth man down the trail on some sort of scouting
trip.

A quick rattle of shouted questions and answers told
him that this was the outlaw scout. It was simple
enough to hear what he was shouting to the others.
Their intended victims were in sight. Two wagons with
an escort of soldiers from Fort Union. The soldiers
were to be wiped out at the first volley. Various ambushers were given their precise targets so that there
would be no useless bullets fired in duplication. They
were to wait until the first trooper in the escort was
opposite Flood's position. Then each ambusher would
fire at a target directly in front of him. No horses were
to be killed unless something went wrong and there
was a runaway. Drivers were to be shot down as soon

as the soldiers were disposed of. Then the rest were to be wiped out.

"Very good ambushers, these," Luis muttered grimly. "They have had much practice, I think. And they have heard our famous saying, *Los muertos no hablan.*"

"Very famous," Baird agreed in much the same tone. " 'Dead men tell no tales' is our version. Who is giving the orders? Oakes?"

"I do not know Oakes by sight. I wondered if it might not be Captain Madison."

"Nobody out there looks like Madison. Have you thought that the order to wipe out the guards means they plan to kill a lot of New Mexican militia at the first volley? Surely you have cousins . . ."

Suddenly the New Mexican grinned. "Ethan makes jokes—but this is something to consider. Also I am concerned about your messenger. I think we must disobey orders. I hope you will explain to Ethan."

He was moving as he hissed the words, inching down the gentle slope on his belly so as to keep the rocks between himself and the nearest of the ambushers. Baird smiled briefly at the young fellow's whimsy but prepared to take an active part in the oncoming fight. He would be alone on this flank but he had good weapons. He had to make good use of them.

He examined the Colt first, checking its action and loads to make certain that sand hadn't fouled the action. Then he put fresh caps on the nipples and laid it close at hand. After that he gave the Sharps a close scrutiny, working the breech mechanism for a quick peek to see that the knife-edge of the breechblock had properly sliced off a bit of the cartridge to expose the powder. It pleased him to see that the move hadn't pulled the Maynard primer out of place. The weapons were ready. He hoped he would be the same.

He sighted tentatively along the carbine barrel, trying to get the feel of the ugly weapon. It occurred to him that he had never fired a shot at a human being, his military service prior to his resignation having been a matter of engineering work only. During his time with the telegraph company he had not had to take any part in driving off the Sioux raiders who had attacked the work parties. This would be his first fight.

He knew a moment of wonder at his own cold detachment, then he snapped out of the mood, his eyes catching the first hint of movement just a little to the left of the crawling Luis. A man in a ragged brown shirt had risen from a hiding place among the rocks and was swinging a musket to blast a shot straight down into the New Mexican's back. Baird already had the carbine raised from his aiming exercise so he lined his sights quickly, his thoughts still finding time for surprise at the presence of this seventh man. Somehow Luis had counted wrong—or the desperadoes had gained a man during the night. He squeezed off his shot just before the musket came all the way around.

Two shots blasted in quick succession and Baird grabbed for the six-gun, trying to see through the smoke. He was ready for a second shot but it obviously was not necessary. Luis was scrambling to his feet and the ambusher had fallen face down among the rocks where his musket had already dropped.

"Hurt?" Baird shouted. More shots were sounding from beyond the rocks now but he didn't try to see who was firing them. He was using the moment to get a fresh cartridge into the carbine.

"He missed," Luis called out. "You did not. Open fire on the others. Ethan and Dirk will need our help."

He scrambled to a spot among the rocks where the dead outlaw lay, firing promptly at the nearest man. Baird turned just in time to see the fellow jump out of his hiding place and start running down toward the trail. He put the carbine sights on him but the shot didn't stop the flight. The man only jumped a little higher as though he had been hit where it stung but didn't cripple. All of the bushwhack party was in full retreat now, evidently too astonished to discover that the attacking force was so small. The men beyond the trail, who could see the field better than the ones under immediate attack, showed as much panic as the others. They were simply racing for their horses, not pausing even to fire a second round of shots in defense.

Luis had cleared the ledge with a couple of long leaps and Baird followed. If Dirk and Warner had moved down toward those outlaw horses, they would be in a bad spot. Six desperate gunmen would be hitting them in a panic which would be as bad as a real attack.

Luis was reloading the big pistol as he ran. Baird simply made a hasty check of the revolver. He didn't propose to fire it again until he had a target that was within range.

They had crossed nearly half of the distance to the concealed horses when the ambushers began to ride out. That was when Baird saw twin puffs of smoke well above the hollow. Evidently Warner and Dirk had not had time to get down to the precarious level. They were simply firing at the outlaws to keep them in panic, the range making it unlikely that they would do any great damage—or be hit themselves.

Luis slowed down then. "They are clear," he panted. "Our men need no help."

The two men halted side by side, watching the six riders whirl into the trail and gallop away to the north. Baird studied them as best he could, reaffirming his earlier opinion that Joe Madison was not one of them. "I'm afraid we didn't get Flood," he said finally.

"It could not be helped. Thank you for saving me back there. I did not count very good, I think."

"Forget it. That fellow surprised us both."

"Ethan and Dirk will have much to say about ruining the attack. I hope you can explain to suit them. I go now to speak with the wagon people. They must be told that we are not of the enemy."

Baird saw the little grin which quirked at the corners of the boy's mouth. "Afraid to face Ethan, are you? Go ahead, coward!"

A broad smile came then. "There is no need to tell that we planned to warn the wagons. It can be our little secret." Then he was hurrying away down the slope.

Warner and Dirk came into sight then, both of them shouting angry questions about the trap having been sprung too soon. Warner was doing most of the yelling and Baird found himself wondering why Vermonters were always considered to be so sparing of words. Warner wasn't sparing any now.

Baird moved across to meet them, making no reply until they were closer—and out of breath. It seemed that Warner was mostly upset about not having his orders obeyed. Dirk was bitter over the escape of Jeremiah Flood. When Baird got into the talk, he put on a show of anger to match that of the others. "Damn it, Warner! Don't you think I'm just as mad as you are? I wanted to get a prisoner out of that gang. Maybe I could have found out a few things."

"Then why in hell did you let it bust loose too soon?"

"We didn't have any choice. Luis could only count five men, but when that rider came up the trail he figured that the whole party was where we could see 'em. We moved down along the rocks to a better position and a seventh man popped up. I suppose the rider we saw was just joining the others but that's not important now. The big point is that this extra man had Luis dead to right—with Luis not even seeing him. I had to shoot the jigger."

Warner's anger seemed to fade. "Ye mean he was about to kill Luis?"

"That's what I'm trying to say."

"Then it couldn't be helped. What's Luis doin' now?"

"He's on his way to tell the wagon people what happened here. I guess you heard that rider yell about

militiamen with the wagons. Luis figures they'll be
edgy at hearing the shots, so he wants to talk with
'em."

Warner nodded. "Troops outa Fort Union will be
Mex militia. Luis is the one to handle 'em. Likely
enough he'll have some of his chili-pepper cousins a-
mong 'em. He ones, that is."

The joke seemed to take away the remnants of his
anger so Baird broke in to ask, "How about coming
over here to see if you know the dead man? It might
tell us something to identify him."

"We'd oughta bring the hosses up fust. Them polecats might swing around to the rear and steal 'em.
Dirk, ye kin handle all of 'em by yerself. Bring 'em
across while I'm takin' a peek at Baird's outlaw."

The blond youth hurried away without comment.
He was still clearly disappointed at the failure to take
Flood, but there was no point in talk now.

Baird led the way across toward the rocks, pausing
by the junipers where one of the ambushers had been
hiding. "I think I nicked this one when he started to
run," he explained to Warner. "I wondered if there
might be any blood spots."

"Ye hit the bastard," Warner growled, pointing to
the gravel. "It sure as hell didn't slow him down much.
They was all runnin' mighty fast when they got where
we could see 'em. It's gonna be one hell of a chore to
git 'em now that they've been skeered like this."

"Then you intend to continue chasing them even
though we're outnumbered?"

The narrowed eyes studied him in a hard stare that
was both grim and amused. "Countin' yerself in, are
ye? Then ye'd better know that we ain't givin' up on
'em. Them bastards bushwhacked our men. We'll git
'em!"

They went across to where the dead ambusher lay
across the top of a jagged rock. The fellow had not
been a very handsome creature in life. In death he was
grotesque, the thick beard and accumulated dirt mak-

ing it difficult to judge his true facial appearance. The carbine slug had left a huge bloody patch and the angle of the body had caused the blood to drain into the matted beard.

Warner rolled him free of the rock and took a long look. "Never seen him before. Did you?"

"No. Not that it would be likely. I'm a stranger in these parts, remember?"

Something in his tone made the older man look around quickly. "Don't git to feelin' squirmish because ye shot the bastard. It was him or Luis, wasn't it?"

"Yes. I have no regrets."

"Don't be gittin' none! Likely he helped massacree them friends of our'n back in the scrub country. See if ye kin tell anything about him by the gun. I'll go through his pockets."

A quick search told them nothing. There was only a jackknife and the remnants of a plug of trade tobacco. The musket was the usual government issue Springfield. Hundreds of them, of one model or another, had been removed from forts and arsenals during the period of mass desertions. It meant nothing.

"Leave him where he's at," Warner ordered gruffly. "If'n his gang don't come back to bury him, the varmints will do the job. Let's git on down there and see what kind o' nonsense Luis is up to now." His voice had turned hard again as though to remind Baird that no matter what the excuse had been, they had failed in their objective. The outlaw band had not been seriously weakened—and the traitorous Flood was still unpunished.

They were working their way down along the rocks when Baird said quietly, "I don't think Joe Madison was with that crowd. I couldn't see anybody who was even close to his description."

"Flood was there!" Warner snapped. "Mebbe ye're keen on findin' out about this Madison jigger. I ain't. It's Flood I'm gonna git!"

Baird didn't like the sound of it. His own chances of doing his job were going to be small enough, even with the help of the Colorado scouts. If they decided to go off on a chase of their own private enemy— He didn't even let himself finish the thought. Somehow he had to keep them on the trail of the bigger game.

Dirk was coming down the ridge with the string of horses when Baird and Warner moved into the trail from which they could see down the rutted path to the south. A little cavalcade had halted there, apparently at the sound of firing. A cluster of men in blue uniforms surrounded Luis, one of them talking volubly—and gesturing in true Latin style. The others did not seem to be showing any great interest. All of them wore infantry uniforms but were well mounted and armed with cavalry carbines. It was only on more careful observation that Baird observed the one real variation in uniforms. Five of the troopers were barefooted, two had moccasins thrust into huge leather stirrups. The officer who was doing the talking wore high boots which must have been given a fine polish during the night. The dust of the morning hadn't even begun to cover the finish.

"Militia outa Santy Fee," Warner growled. "Fort Union ain't got nothin' else, I reckon. Likely they ain't willin' to move into country where there's been shootin'."

Baird grinned thinly at this open show of prejudice. "I hear they did their share at the Apache Canyon fight."

"Oh, some of 'em's good fighters—when their officers give 'em a chance," Warner said grudgingly. "Fer that matter, it was the same with our boys. In that Apache Canyon business both sides threw away chances to win because stupid officers didn't use the men what was anxious to git into the fight. Ye might say we beat Sibley because his commanders was even stupider'n our'n."

"That's different, anyway," Baird commented dry-

ly. "Back east it has generally been the other way
around. The Confederates win most of the battles
because the Union command has a monopoly of the
first-class stupidity."

"Let's see what the hell Luis is tryin' to do," Warner
growled irritably. "With all that talk ye might think
he was organizin' a fandango or somethin'."

"Probably cousins," Baird commented. "He ones."

As he spoke, he was trying to appraise the wagons
which had halted behind the knot of militiamen. One
wagon partly concealed the other but he was sure
that there were only two. The first was a heavy freight
wagon which had been fitted with bows and canvas to
give it something of the Conestoga appearance. A
small man sat immobile on the driver's seat as though
totally disinterested in the whole proceeding. Behind
him a round female face showed. A stout woman was
glaring at the scene ahead, her impatience showing
even at this distance.

The second wagon was only partly visible, but it
was smaller, apparently the sort of vehicle which the
army called an ambulance but which was used as a
carryall by ranchers and farmers and called by a variety of names. Its occupants were not visible behind
the larger wagon.

Dirk overtook them with the horses and they swung
into their saddles, Baird commenting, "Only two wagons but with seven men and an officer as escort. I
wonder why the outlaw gang was so anxious to wipe
'em out?"

"I never thought about that," Warner muttered.
"If'n they'd been grabbin' fer wimmen I'd understand.
These outlaw bastards deal with the Comanches
sometimes—and Comanches kinda hanker after white
wimmen."

"I've only seen one woman so far—and they didn't
plan on taking prisoners. You heard their orders."

"That's what puzzles me. Likewise I can't see 'em
recruitin' Jerry Flood fer that kind of a deal."

"Ask Luis," Dirk broke in. "He oughta have the whole yarn by this time. They been doin' enough talkin'."

Baird didn't say anything. He was trying to do some guessing on his own part. This was not exactly the way he had expected the government messenger to arrive but maybe this was the strategy. Other travelers could serve as a sort of disguise. That at least might have been the intention. The ambush attempt suggested that the enemy had not been fooled.

Chapter 5

The woman Baird had noticed behind the wagon driver came at this point into full view. She was a big woman, perhaps in her fifties, and the business of clambering to the wagon seat seemed to be quite an effort for her. The driver made no effort to help, but Baird caught a glimpse of a pretty blonde woman giving her a boost from the rear.

Warner apparently hadn't noticed the blonde for he made no comment. Instead he muttered uneasily, "That Mex officer looks too damned fancy to me. Between him and that fat woman this here's gonna git a mite sticky. Mebbe I ought let ye handle it; ye used to be an officer."

Baird still wasn't ready to admit that he had been recommissioned. It looked like a far better strategy to keep Warner in a position of responsibility. "Corporal," he said solemnly, "I don't think we should try to deceive them. You are the only one here who has official status. You'll have to handle it."

"Then be ready to back me up, dammit! I'm fixin' to give that jack-a-dandy lieutenant partickler hell fer not tryin' to chase them outlaws."

"Save your breath," Baird advised, speaking through tight lips as they drew within earshot of the militiamen. "I don't think he speaks English. Anyway, these New Mexican troops have a happy knack of doing as they damn please, I understand. Let Luis handle it."

They let Luis continue with his harangue and the young fellow began to make his explanations as they drew to a halt. "I regret, Corporal Warner," he said formally, "that this idiot of a lieutenant would not move forward to support us. My regret is all the more deep because he is is my cousin. Because he is of a branch of the family far more wealthy than my own he would not take a suggestion from me. So he has permitted outlaws to escape. He says only that he has a duty to escort wagons, not to pursue outlaws."

"Don't try to git funny," Warner growled. "I take it yer cousin don't talk American or ye wouldn't be gittin' so damned smart."

Luis winked broadly, obviously enjoying the game he was playing. "My cousin speaks no English. He is stupid in many other ways, far more stupid than the ignorant peons he leads. If you have anything to say to him, Corporal, I will be happy to translate."

Baird had a feeling that one of the barefooted soldiers understood English well enough to be enjoying what he was hearing. Probably Luis knew it. He could be sure that his insults about the lieutenant would soon be known among the soldiers.

The low comedy came at that moment to an abrupt end. From the seat of the big wagon the stout woman shrilled, "Will you stupid Yankees stop delaying this wagon! We have been kept waiting enough already!" Her voice was so sharp with impatience that the southern accent almost failed to show through. The scrawny little driver at her side hunched his shoulders a little as though expecting the next verbal attack to be aimed at him and Baird decided that the little man had been through this sort of thing before.

"You're the Yankee, Ethan," he told Warner in an

undertone. "I'd say that the lady was a bit out of patience with somebody—probably you."

"Damn!" Warner grumbled. "Fust off we git a jim-dandy lieutenant what can't talk the language and now we have to run afoul of a female Rebel windbag! I'd rather fight outlaws."

"You don't have a choice," Baird murmured.

Warner seemed to pull himself together. Then he kneed his horse forward through the open ranks of the escort. He even touched his hat in a sort of informal salute as he addressed the stout woman with vast formality. "I'm Coporal Warner, Fust Colorado Cavalry," he announced without a trace of expression on his bewhiskered face. "We're on a scout patrol and we seen a gang o' brash apes fixin' to waylay yer wagons. We busted up the ambush. We're plumb sorry we didn't do it jest the way ye think it oughta been done."

"Don't try to sound so heroic!" she snapped. "I know very well that the outlaws in this area are a lot of petty thieves. There could be no reason for such creatures to arrange an ambush when the victims were to be only women and their scant property."

"Mebbe they didn't know who it was what was comin', ma'am," Ethan replied in that same deceptively humble tone. "It coulda been a mistake." He scratched his head slowly for a minute and then added, "But mebbe they knowed what they was doin'. Wimmen are a mite skeerce along the Cimarron. The Comanches will hand over quite a passel o' furs in a swap fer a nice fat one."

She gulped, sputtered, reddened—and finally came out with something incoherent about "insolent Yankees." At that point Luis intervened to ride in beside Warner and hand him a packet of papers. "These are for you, Corporal," he announced with the same determined formality he had been assuming. "My good cousin, the brave and stupid lieutenant, tells me that these are his orders. He now transfers them to you."

It was Warner's turn to be speechless. Finally he demanded, "What the hell reason should he give 'em to me? What's in 'em?"

"Read 'em," Baird suggested dryly.

"Don't git so damned smart. The lingo's too damned fancy fer me. Take 'em and tell me what they say."

Baird scanned the closely written pages that were thrust at him, taking plenty of time in wading through the military verbiage. He realized that all talk had stopped. Everyone was watching him, waiting for him to comment. Even the stout woman on the wagon seemed to think that this was no time for her to say more.

"I'll boil it down," he told Ethan when he had it well in mind. "It seems that this first wagon is carrying two ladies who are to be escorted to St. Louis and then down the Mississippi through the Confederate lines. One of them is Mrs. Margaretta Haislip, wife of a Colonel Haislip who resigned his commission last year because he felt his primary loyalty was to the State of Alabama. The second is Mrs. Rowena Davenport, wife of Captain Davenport, likewise resigned—for the same reason except that it's Georgia instead of Alabama. Lieutenant Garcia is ordered to escort the ladies with proper diligence northward from Fort Union along the Cimarron Trail until he can turn them over to the next available force of Union troops. That detachment is to continue the relay process and so on to the Mississippi. I take it that Lieutenant Garcia thinks that a body of Colorado Cavalry is the proper relief force for his purpose."

Warner pointed a bony finger at Luis. "Tell that stupid cousin o' your'n that we ain't Union troops, dammit! Tell him we're Colorado militia! Tell him we ain't even got no business here. Mebbe we ain't even in Colorado. Sure as hell we ain't supposed to be draggin' no Reb wimmen over into Kansas!"

"I might have expected such a reaction," the stout woman declared angrily. "Let me inform you that I am Mrs. Haislip. I shall certainly report this gross breach of faith when I reach the proper authorities. Bad manners and inattention to duty is no more than I would expect of Yankees, but these are formal orders."

Warner stared hard for a long minute. Then he said clearly, "I'm a Yankee, all right, ma'am. A New England Yankee. Up where I hail from we useta have duckin' stools fer fat witches what don't stop blabbin'. Down this way we kin always peddle 'em to the Comanches. Don't tempt me!"

Baird had been doing some fast thinking while the barbs were exchanged. He didn't like the prospect of his only allies being drafted into a job which would take them out of the dangerous area, but he still had a feeling that there was more to this wagon business than appeared on the surface. Why had two Confederate women been sent up the Cimarron Trail instead of the Raton Pass route? If there was a real reason behind the move, he had to find out what it was.

"Your orders mention two women," he reminded Ethan. "They're both in the first wagon. We'd better find out what that second wagon means."

"Go do it," Warner growled crossly. "I got enough to worry about right here."

Mrs. Haislip tried to stop him as he swung out around her wagon. "You seem to carry some authority, young man. Can't you beat some sense or manners into that dirty old man?"

He tipped his dusty hat with careful politeness. "No, ma'am. The dirty old man is boss over us dirty younger men. You'd better do as he says." Then he was swinging out to a point where he could see the other vehicle. It was a pleasant move. The woman handling the lines on the rear wagon was a distinct improvement over Mrs. Haislip.

He studied her openly as he rode around past the big wagon with the extra horses tied at its tailgate. She was quietly dressed in a gray gown which only partly concealed a well-rounded figure. She wore no bonnet, the dark brown hair braided into an arrangement aimed at the practical needs of hard travel. It was still very attractive and made Baird uneasily conscious of his own disreputable appearance. He guessed that the woman might be anywhere between twenty-five and thirty-five, but he never had been very good at such guesses so he didn't consider the point very long. The interesting point was that she had alert gray eyes, a slightly tilted nose and a very nice complexion. He liked everything he saw.

"Any problems back here, ma'am?" he inquired, dabbing a hand toward his hat brim.

"No more than up front, soldier," she replied. The gray eyes were studying him with a frankness which matched his own. "I heard the talk up there. Are we in any great danger?" She didn't seem worried—and her voice was definitely not southern.

"No danger at the moment," he assured her. "We can't quite figure out why a gang of deserters and outlaws would try to waylay wagons that don't seem to be carrying anything valuable."

Her glance became a trifle quizzical. "You think women are not valuable? I'm sure Mrs. Davenport may feel rather hurt at that." Somehow she managed to indicate that the lady in question had appeared at the wagon which was now behind him.

He turned in the saddle to see that the blonde he had seen helping Mrs. Haislip had now moved to the rear of the big vehicle and was eyeing him with open interest. He saw that she was also young enough to be interesting, perhaps not as old as the brunette. She had evidently made some attempt to arrange her mass of pale hair into something just a trifle too ornate for wagon travel but there was nothing wrong with the final result. Her smile came quickly as he looked around. "I think Mrs. Haislip has met her match," she called softly, the drawl of the deep South clear in her tones. "I hope he is only trying to frighten her with that talk of Comanches."

"No need to scare people, ma'am," Baird told her gravely. "We don't have any shortage of things to be scared about."

Then he swung back to the other woman. "I think you know what I had in mind. Nothing personal. Which is why I rode around the big wagon. Corporal Warner is a mite bothered. This is not the job he was sent down here to handle. He's not sure yet just what it means. Those orders don't even mention a third woman."

"I suppose you're asking me to explain myself," she said quietly. "Be assured that I can identify myself properly and that I am not some dangerous enemy. I simply attached myself to the convoy because it was convenient. I have papers which you may examine, if you wish. I am Mrs. Patience Rexford. I have been a resident of Santa Fe for nearly seven years. My husband passed away last year and I wish to return east to join relatives there." The words came out almost casually. She was simply explaining, asking no favors.

The way she kept her eyes on him as she spoke suggested that she was watching closely for some re-action. It gave him an idea which at first seemed too ridiculous to believe. He nodded slowly and then asked, "Anybody else traveling in your wagon?"

"No one. I am quite alone."

This time he felt sure that she put just a shade of extra meaning into the words so he decided to make a try. "Seems like a shame," he said, wondering if he sounded as silly as he felt. This was going to be a pretty asinine remark but he didn't dare come out too openly with the other woman listening. "Two ladies in the first wagon. Oughta be two in this one. It would sorta balance things up."

She met his look squarely. "Isn't that a rather foolish remark?"

He was about to offer some sort of apology when he

noticed the slight movement of her hands. She had been sitting on the wagon seat, still holding the reins of her team. Now he saw that she had slipped the leathers through her fingers so that only two fingers of each hand showed. It was definitely the two and two sign, given so that only someone watching for it would notice.

He dismounted without a word, his manner brusque as he tied his horse to a wagon wheel and said, "I'd better take a look at your papers, ma'am. The Corporal will want to know about you."

She handed over an envelope which contained such commonplace documents as bills of sale for the horses and the wagon, a marriage certificate and some receipted bills from a shop in Santa Fe. Everything fitted with what she had first told him but he held up one paper as though questioning it. As she leaned over to look, he murmured, "When did you join the Loyal League?"

She pointed to the paper as though explaining something but her actual words were, "I didn't. I joined the Union League. And we'd better omit the handshake and the other statement. Mrs. Davenport isn't missing a bit of this."

He nodded, handed back the envelope as though satisfied, and turned to untie his horse. "By the way, I'm Tom Baird, temporarily attached to the Colorado scouts." That should give her hint enough without telling Mrs. Davenport anything.

Before he could make another move he heard sharp commands being shouted in Spanish. Mrs. Haislip was making shrill objections to something but the point of the objection was not immediately clear.

Then Mrs. Rexford said, "Our New Mexican friends are about to leave us. Or did you already understand what the lieutenant was saying?"

He shook his head. "No Spanish, ma'am. I guess he must have won his argument with Corporal Warner."

"I don't believe he gave Corporal Warner any choice. To be fair about it, he is being rather smart. Our wagons carry a fair supply of water which we dole out to the stock. Mounted troops do not have such an advantage. When we crossed the Cimarron it was dry except for stagnant puddles and the escort must consider that point. They return because there is no water for them."

"No other reason?" Baird asked with a crooked grin.

The lady smiled. "It may not be charitable to mention it but I'm afraid Lieutenant Garcia has been quite uneasy since he heard the sound of gunfire. I think he was very happy to find someone he could use as his excuse for being relieved of this duty."

The New Mexican militia came around past the big wagon, the dapper lieutenant riding in the lead with a definite show of pompousness. He saluted Mrs. Rexford with great formality; Baird was surprised to see how the men behind him followed his example in their own individual styles. Most of them called formal farewells in courteous Spanish but two or three of them used a more familiar, *"Adios,* Señora Rey." It was pretty easy to see that they knew her, liked her, and respected her.

"You seem to have been among friends," he commented as he stood by his waiting horse. He wasn't sure what she might want to tell him but it seemed as though he ought to give her some excuse for talking.

"I am grateful that they feel so," she said soberly. "Many of them have lived in Santa Fe. They knew my husband as a friend of their people. They called him El Doctor Rey so I became Señora Rey." Her smile became a little broader as she added, "I'd better explain that his name was not Ray. This is R-e-y and is the Spanish equivalent of Rex as in Rexford. We felt rather flattered by it. There was something in it that tried to show their gratitude and friendship."

Baird wanted to press for a little more explanation

but Warner's angry bellow sounded from the front. "Let's git this outfit rollin'! Luis, git on up ahead and keep an eye skinned fer them bushwhackin' polecats. Dirk, wake up that driver and git him on the job. Where the hell's Baird?"

"I think Corporal Warner has accepted the job, ladies," Baird said as he climbed into the saddle, a wave of his hand serving as a salute to both of them. "I hope you will be pleased with the efforts of the First Colorado." Then he rode forward to where Warner was leading off and Dirk was grumbling at the silent little man on the wagon seat. Mrs. Haislip had evidently retired behind the canvas to sulk.

Chapter 6

For a few minutes Baird rode beside Warner without either of them saying a word. Warner was grumbling under his breath and Baird was trying to think. He knew that surprise had made him jump to a conclusion and now he wasn't sure that he had not made a serious mistake. Membership in the Loyal League did not necessarily mean that Mrs. Rexford was the expected messenger. Many civilian members of the League had no official duties.

Finally Warner growled, "What did ye find out about that other wagon?"

"There's another woman in it. She gave me the League sign but I couldn't talk to her. The blonde Reb was watching us."

"Ye think she's yer messenger?"

"I've just been wondering. I'll have to find out—but I guess there's no real rush. Now that we've got the escort duty there'll be time."

"What the hell else could I do but take it? That Mex lieutenant claimed that his orders were to turn the chore over to the first troops he met. I kinda figger somebody was expectin' him to run across a patrol outa Fort Larned but I couldn't argy when we didn't talk the same language. God knows what that damned Luis translated. He was so full o' bein' a joker that there ain't no tellin' what he said."

"Mrs. Rexford—that's the woman in the second wagon—told me that the militiamen were in a bad way for water. They wanted to turn back to save their horses. She speaks Spanish, by the way."

"Likely they didn't want to hear no more shootin'!" Warner grunted.

"Do you figure to escort the wagons all the way to Fort Larned? Assuming that nobody else shows up."

"Looks like there ain't nobody else goin' to do it."

"What about your friend Flood?"

Warner gave him a sidelong glance. "I was kinda figgerin' on him," he said with what was almost a chuckle. "Him and his friends was plumb itchin' to git at these wagons. I kinda look fer 'em to try again. Mebbe it's gonna be easier to toll him in than to chase him."

"Suppose he picks up some more men? That crowd isn't the only outlaw gang in the territory."

"That's a risk we're gonna have to take. I kinda work it out thisaway. Them ornery bastards ain't sure how much of an enemy they've got. When we hit 'em a spell ago, they lit out so fast that they didn't have time to see how many of us was movin' in. One of 'em is sure enough goin' to report seein' one stranger in the lot—you. They might git to thinkin' that ye've got more with ye. And they ain't goin' to know fer a spell yit that the Mex militia ain't still comin' along. Mebbe we kin bluff 'em out 'til we git some help."

"From Fort Larned?"

"Hell! I dunno. I ain't even sure what I oughta be doin'. I ain't sure I'm still in Colorado. Likely enough I ain't got any right to herd these wagons into Kansas. But I'm stubborn. If that bastard of a Flood is fixin' to meddle with this outfit—and went to the trouble o' murderin' some o' my friends to do it—then I'm fixin' to meddle with his meddlin'. Me and the boys have got a axe to grind with him. We'd jest as soon grind it in Kansas as in Colorado."

"Suits me fine," Baird told him. "Now tell me something. Has Luis spent any time lately among his various relatives around Santa Fe?"

"Sure. He useta handle wagons in the trade. Why?"

"I need to know more about this Rexford woman. The New Mex boys were mighty polite when they passed her. I gather that she's the widow of a Santa Fe doctor who died recently. I hoped Luis might tell me more about her before I get into any more talk with her. I can't afford to spill any secrets if she's not the agent I'm supposed to meet."

"Then stop wastin' yer time with me," Warner snapped with a show of irritation. "Git up ahead there and talk to Luis. We oughta have more'n one man ridin' point anyhow."

He overtook Luis quickly enough, nodding as the New Mexican pointed to the tracks of galloping horses. The retreating ambushers had followed the half-obliterated wagon ruts in their retreat. They were running away but they would be in position for another strike, probably another ambush attempt.

"We've been trying to figure out what these fellows wanted," Baird said as he swung in beside the other man. "That ambush was planned ahead of time. The man who came along with the final word about the approach of the wagons was not with the other six when they stopped at that point. They went to a lot of trouble to hit those wagons. Why?"

"Loot?"

"I don't think so. There's a woman in the second wagon who says her name is Patience Rexford. Do you know her?"

The swarthy face broke into a smile. "A fine lady. My people owe her much. Also they owe much to her husband who died last spring."

"Any chance she might be the reason for that ambush attempt?"

Luis shook his head. "It does not sound sensible to me. Why do you ask?"

"There's got to be some explanation. That ambush was planned ahead of time. All signs point to that. Several men were sent to do the job. They had orders for a complete wipeout. Why?"

"I see what you mean. Some of them came all the way from the Purgatory. Murder without plunder is not the outlaw way. I have been puzzled by it."

"Did any of your Santa Fe militiamen say anything that would give you a hint of any kind of trouble?"

"No. I think maybe I was too anxious to make fun of my cousin. He has always looked down on my part of the family. Today I had a chance to get even, you might say. Two of his men speak enough English so that I could be sure my words would be reported to the others. For their private amusement, of course. I think I should have asked questions instead of making jokes."

"Maybe they didn't know anything. It just seemed to me that they were in a mighty big hurry to get away."

"That I can defend," Luis told him seriously. "A while ago I hinted that it was cowardice on my cousin's part. Now I tell you that he was being prudent. Water was of great concern. At the crossing of the Cimarron they dug holes and let them fill with bad water so that their horses might drink. They will lose the animals if they do not get more water soon. The Cimarron is the only likely place. They had to go back. Also they were already farther from Fort Union than such escorts generally ride. I wondered why they took the risk. Now I know. If Senora Rey—Mrs. Rexford, that is—occupies the other wagon, our people would take many risks to give her protection."

He broke off to point to the tracks they had been following. The outlaws had left the regular trail here and had swung northwest along the general line of a crooked little arroyo. "Very bad country over there,"

Luis said. "Some hills and many rocks. Also some bad water but better than no water. Outlaws use it for hiding many times."

"Would this crowd know about it? They came from along the Purgatory, didn't they?"

"Flood would know. Also this seventh man who was here. Probably he would know." He shook his head soberly as he added, "And I do not like the way they leave the open trail. They do not care if we know where they go. Perhaps they expect to find other outlaws there, so many that it will not matter if someone follows to attack them."

"You make a real cheerful sound," Baird told him with a wry smile. "I think they're going to take another crack at those wagons. Maybe they'll attack in force next time. Should we follow these tracks and make sure they're headed for this outlaw hangout you mentioned?"

"We go far enough to be sure they do not circle for a new attack. Better we should ride apart from each other now. Be alert always."

They followed the tracks for a little over a mile, the sign of retreat always clear. Finally Luis seemed satisfied. "They continue to the rocky hills," he announced. "We go that way. It is a shorter path to meet the wagons. Ethan should know of this."

"He's already expecting that they'll come back. In fact, he's counting on it. Another crack at Flood may be the only thing that's keeping him on the job."

As they rode across country to reach the trail, Luis added a few details to the Rexford story. Doctor and Mrs. Rexford had come to Sante Fe some five years before the outbreak of war. The doctor was sick. It was not the lung trouble which caused many people to come to the dry country but some internal ailment which the doctor understood but could not cure. He was a fine physician. Important people of the community called upon him when they needed help. They must have paid him well, for he made a living without charging any fee to the many poor people he treated. His wife worked with him, partly as nurse and partly to help him along when he had weak spells.

"This is the great puzzle to me," Luis declared as they pulled in along the Cutoff trail to wait for the slowly rolling wagons. "Many people around Santa Fe would gladly commit a murder if the Señora would profit by it. I know of no one who would wish to harm her."

"Do you think the murder intention was aimed at someone else?"

"I do not know. No New Mexicans were among the bandits but they had received orders from south of us. New Mexicans might know about it. It is a puzzle."

"Any reason you can think of why they'd want to murder the other women?"

Luis permitted a flicker of a smile to cross his lips. "In the case of Mrs. Haislip it would not be difficult to imagine. I have not seen the other one."

"Nonsense! You're trying to be funny again. This was a planned operation. Somebody spent some money to get those outlaws over here with no prospect of loot. There's got to be a reason."

He waited while Luis stared silently across the barren sands, then decided that he might as well take the young fellow a little more into his confidence. That was the trouble of having to depend on people when he was not supposed to trust them all the way with secrets. "Is there any chance that Mrs. Rexford could be the government messenger I am supposed to meet?"

Luis shook his head almost automatically. "It could not be, and yet—perhaps it is not so impossible. Doctor Rexford was an important man to those who declared for the Union. Both he and Mrs. Rexford spent much time with our people when they did not know what to do about this war. It was Mrs. Rexford who pointed out that the true enemy of the New Mexican was the Texan. I think she may have had much to do with the failure of Colonel Sibley to recruit troops in New Mexico."

Warner came on ahead of the wagons and they had time to exchange their information and ideas. Warner was willing to accept the theory that some outlaw organization—or Rebel agent—might have tried to arrange the murder of a Federal agent, who might or might not be a woman, but he insisted that the other two were not covering the whole problem.

"What's Flood `doin' in it?" he demanded. "They went to a hell of a lot o' risk to git him. Plannin' to murder seven well-armed fightin' men is a risk. Three of us got away—so the risk is ripe to cause 'em trouble. It means Flood has got to be damned important. They sure as hell didn't need him jest to gun down some wimmen!"

"And they didn't need him to guide them across from the Purgatory," Baird added. "Some of them were out ahead of him and it looks like one man was to meet them here on the Cutoff. That's the one who fouled up our count and spoiled the attack for us." He caught the New Mexican's eye as he said this. It seemed like a good idea to let Luis know that Warner hadn't been told about the attempt to warn the wagons.

"There's got to be somethin' big brewin'," Warner growled. "I wonder if it's somethin' to do with these Reb wimmen?"

"Maybe Mrs. Rexford can tell us. If she's the messenger she must have some kind of information. I'll try to get around to having a real talk with her, casual like. No point in making the others wonder."

"Mebbe ye'll git a chance," Warner told him. "Have ye been noticin' them thunderheads over in the nor' west? We might settle this damned water shortage real soon."

They separated again, Baird and Luis moving ahead as scouts while Warner waited for the wagons to overtake him. The dry heat was beginning to do its daily burn but now it seemed that there was a peculiar stifling quality to it. Breathing became difficult and Baird wondered how the dark-haired woman would be getting along in the pall of dust that the first wagon would be leaving in its wake. He found it easy to think about her, not only because she might have the key to the mystery that was puzzling him but also because it was pleasant to remember the smooth features and the mass of dark hair. Somehow it was a little difficult to remember that she was a widow.

They omitted any noontime halt. It was pretty obvious that Ethan didn't like the look of that growing cloud bank so he was making as much progress as possible while it was practical to keep wagons moving.

Baird watched the clouds almost impatiently as he flanked out to the right, while Luis followed a line closer to those distant hills in the northwest. It seemed to Baird that in the past twenty-four hours he had known only puzzles. If he was going to get any answers from Mrs. Rexford, he wanted to get them soon. Then he might be able to guess just what job was actually ahead of him.

In midafternoon he saw Luis cut sharply back toward the trail so he swung to meet him, suspecting that there was some reason for alarm.

"No sign of them," Luis grinned as they met, reading the unspoken question in Baird's mind. "I want to tell Ethan that there is shelter ahead. I think the wagons can reach it before the storm breaks. Do you think you should scout the left side now?"

Baird smiled. "You don't have to be diplomatic about giving me orders, Luis. When you're the one we depend on—you give the orders. It's likely to be my turn soon enough."

Luis nodded and swung his horse to ride back along the trail. Baird moved into the rough country to the east of the route, scanning every bit of broken terrain for signs of an enemy but very much aware of the speed of those lowering clouds. The storm was coming up fast now, the August heat fading swiftly before the first chill winds. He idled along, getting his slicker roll unfastened and preparing to protect himself from the expected downpour. An hour earlier he would have been happy to get a wetting. Now those winds made the prospect somewhat less pleasant.

He had just crossed a dry wash which probably would become a rushing torrent in the event of a heavy storm when he saw Luis waving for him to return to the trail. The wagons were already crossing the arroyo and he could guess their objective. Not far north of the wash, a line of low bluffs flanked the trail on the left. That would be the shelter Luis had mentioned. It wouldn't be much but it would be better than nothing. For a moment he considered its disadvantages in case of attack but decided that the enemy would not be making any moves during the storm. The wagons would have to get moving again in a hurry to avoid such an attack after the storm passed.

Warner met him as he closed in on the wagons. "We'll rig fer heavy weather. Luis is goin' to look after that fust wagon. Mebbe he'll weasel a bit o' talk outa them Reb women while he's at it. He's smart enough on a chore like that. Now's yer chance to see what ye kin learn from the other one."

"What about the other chores we'll need to do before the storm hits us?"

"Me'n Dirk—and that stupid critter on the fust wagon—kin take care of the rest. Git us some information. I'm gittin' curiouser by the Goddam minute!"

Baird assisted with moving the wagons into close quarters where a rope corral could be set up between them and the bluffs. When the stock was under control he drifted back to where Mrs. Rexford was removing the tops from her water barrels. Out of the corner of his eye he saw that Luis had timed his own moves so that he could go to the assistance of the other two women at the same time. They were trying to put extra lashings on their canvas, obviously aware that it was not a very sturdy rig.

"What can I do to help?" Baird asked the brunette.

"You might help me with this canvas to catch runoff from the wagon. After that Cimarron water I don't want to waste a chance for good water."

The first big drops of rain hit them as they were finishing the chore, so he made his move promptly. With the roar of the wind there was no worry about being overheard. Mrs. Haislip and Mrs. Davenport had already retreated to the interior of their wagon anyway. "Does the name Knowles mean anything to you?" he asked abruptly.

"Spelled with an N?"

"With a K."

She managed a sidelong glance as she bowed her head to the rain. "I expected you to try that question sooner or later—and I hoped it would be sooner. Come on into the wagon. This is the best chance we're likely to get for the kind of talk we need to have."

He boosted her to the wagon seat and followed promptly. "I wonder what your Rebel friends are going to think about this?"

"The worst, of course. At least Mrs. Haislip will. I rather believe Mrs. Davenport will be jealous." She motioned for him to take a seat on some blankets which had been spread on piles of baggage. "Now tell me a few things. Then I'll try to explain several matters to you."

Chapter 7

Baird eased out of his slicker, trying to avoid brushing the raindrops on the neat piles of clothing all around him. The wagon was fairly snug against the rain, but it was rather cramped for two people and the considerable baggage. He found it just a trifle disconcerting to be holding a sort of council of war in a traveling boudoir. "What is your question, ma'am?" he asked, giving her a brief smile in recognition of her attempt to set him at ease with that show of wry humor.

"Don't call me ma'am! I hate it. Maybe you should start right now using Pat. My friends do. I have a suspicion that we are going to be working together for some little time."

He nodded. "Could be. And mighty nice for me."

"Thank you. Now can we get down to business?"

"Fine. What's your question?"

"Really two of them. How far is it to Fort Larned? How soon can we expect help from there?"

"I'll answer the last one first. Probably we won't get any help from there. I stopped there when I was swinging around toward Fort Bent. I had a paper from both Knowles and from the Governor of Colorado asking them to give me a few soldiers for a scouting expedition. The commandant refused. His garrison was so ridiculously small that he did not even dare to send out guards with army supply wagons. In the event of even a small Indian raid he could not hope to hold the post."

She leaned closer as the storm really began to roar. "I was afraid of that. I've heard reports. How far?"

"I don't know. I'm new in these parts but my memory of the map and a few remarks I've heard today would make me think that we're about two-thirds of the way from Fort Union to the Arkansas River."

"I assume that you were sent to meet me?"

"Along with several other errands. Nobody bothered to tell me that the messenger would be a most attractive lady. Likely enough they don't put that kind of information into telegraph messages."

"You don't need to bother with compliments. This is a very serious situation, I'm afraid."

"Do you carry written reports of any sort?"

"No. I was instructed not to do so. Now that there has been a definite attempt to stop these wagons—and I interpret that effort as an attempt to stop me—I think it would be very well if I told you everything that I now know."

She paused, letting a peal of thunder die away into the sound of hammering rain. "It will be a relief to confide in someone. When they gave me that initiation and the secret signs and words I was almost amused. It seemed like unnecessary play-acting. When I began to find the amount of treason which is corrupting the frontier posts, I began to understand the necessity for loyal people being able to recognize each other. Now I'm doubly glad to have it so."

"Is the treason out here really so bad?"

"I'm afraid so. Many honorable southern officers resigned their commissions and went home at the outbreak of war, feeling the greater loyalty to their states. Others remained at their posts, deliberately attempting to damage the Union by treasonable methods from the inside."

Another roll of thunder forced a break and then she went on, "I don't think there is any doubt but what the disaster at Val Verde was due to deliberate issuing of false orders by supposedly loyal officers. Sibley was able to take Santa Fe without a bit of trouble. He found difficulty only when he began to find loyal militia facing him. Your Colorado men undoubtedly saved Fort Union. Militia may not be efficient but they're generally loyal."

"Not always," he told her grimly. "This Colorado detachment I happened to meet was in the right place to break up the ambush attempt simply because they were carrying out an attempt at revenge on one of their men who has just turned traitor. I do not belong to the Colorado group, as I think I hinted. My original orders are from Washington. I am supposed to have a commission as captain but the papers haven't caught up with me yet."

"Perhaps you should tell me just what your purpose is," she told him. "It is possible that I can help."

"I was hoping for that. My official story—which I shall tell to your friends in the other wagon—is that I was sent here to see if a man named Madison is still operating in this part of the territory. I knew Joe Madison when we were at the Academy together. I'm supposed to be able to recognize him if he's here. The government wants to know whether a Confederate officer is behind the talk of brewing trouble, or whether the Madison name is being used as a false trail of some kind."

She nodded soberly, waiting for a howling gust to subside. Then she said, "I've heard the Madison talk. My best informants have never seen him. I think he left the area last year."

"Good. Now let me mention one thing before I forget it. Corporal Warner is a member of the Loyal League. The other two men are not, but I feel that they are to be trusted. As a matter of fact, I've got to trust them with quite a bit of rather dangerous information. They're the only help I can get."

"Then I'd better tell you what I know. You can decide how much of it to share with the other men. Have you heard any reports of a group known as the Pecos Volunteers?"

He turned to stare in the semidarkness. "So they're not imaginary! What about Cimarron Thunder?"

"I'm coming to that. It would seem that this is not as secret as I thought."

"Secret enough. Washington has had the terms passed along. They don't know what to believe. That's my real job here. To find out."

"Very well. I can supply a bit of it. You know about the arms that were supposed to have been left on the Pecos when Sibley had to retreat down the Rio Grande?"

"I know the rumor."

"It is undoubtedly true. Sibley himself seems to have been greatly concerned over the fact that when this Pecos detachment rejoined him east of El Paso, they reported a number of desertions. Eight men had disappeared from the retreating column and there was a suspicion that they intended to return to the arms cache with criminal plans.

"The people who knew the story disagreed as to what happened after that. One theory is that a Confederate fanatic planned to form a guerrilla army, seize the arms, and march into Colorado in an attempt to do what Sibley had failed to do. This lunatic has been condemning Confederate Commissioner Pike for not trying to turn Indian treaties into alliances for war. He plans to recruit savages and arm them from that cache."

Baird shook his head, leaning toward her so that he did not have to shout above the storm. "Scare talk. People on the frontier are always imagining Indian wars, not that anybody can blame them. We've talked

it over and we think William Bent can hold the
Cheyennes in line, perhaps the Arapahoes also. The
Kiowas and Comanches won't help Texans."

"You have just explained the true danger," she
argued. "People fear an Indian uprising. They almost
expect one. If this maniac collects a few renegades
and sends them against the settlers, there will be immediate panic. Fear will stimulate imagination and
peaceful tribes will be blamed. It has happened many
times before. With so much tension all around us it
will take almost nothing to start a full-scale Indian
war. You know what that will mean. The federal
government will have to withdraw troops from the
Mississippi. It will ruin offensive plans already in
motion. I think it is quite possible that Confederate
officials might encourage this kind of madness simply
because it will relieve the pressure on their armies."

Baird studied her frankly in the gloom. It seemed
odd to have this mild-looking young woman talking
so knowingly in military terms. "It might happen that
way," he acknowledged as a heavy blast of wind
rocked the wagon. "One incident to get the panic
started and the whole west would be in flames. Do you
have any real evidence that such a plan exists?"

Before she could reply, there was another gust
which threatened to overturn the wagon. Baird had
the ridiculous feeling that only the heavy pounding of
the rain was keeping the wagon from going over.
Suddenly part of the curtain which blocked off the
front tore loose and the rain began to drive in on
them. Baird grabbed at the wildly flapping canvas and
managed to haul it down so that it still offered a little
shelter. "Got any rope handy?" he shouted above the
noise. "I'll go outside and lash it into place while you
hold it."

She practically burrowed under him to reach a
little storage box, but came up promptly with a hank
of light rope. "You'll have to get a knot tied in the

corner of the canvas," she panted. "The fastener has torn loose."

"Put the knot in it now while I hold it. We'll attach the rope also. You can pass it out to me when we're ready."

She was almost in his lap as they worked together at the task and he decided that there were certain advantages connected with being in a mess like this one.

She slid hastily back to the place she had been occupying. "Just hold it there," she suggested. "You'll get soaked if you go outside."

"I'm soaked already. Get ready to shove the rope out."

It took a little time, Mrs. Rexford holding the canvas and Baird trying to secure it outside, but finally they managed to restore some semblance of shelter to the wagon's front end. Then he climbed back into the interior, dripping all over everything. "Sorry I'm messing up the place," he told her. "And maybe it wasn't necessary. The storm's passing. There's bright sky behind the bluffs already. You'd better finish what you had to tell me while I still have an excuse for staying here."

She replied hastily as though trying hard to divert his attention from the way the wet gown was clinging to her very shapely figure. It was a wasted effort. Baird was quite capable of listening and enjoying the scenery at the same time. "There are two other beliefs as to what is being planned. One is that another Confederate invasion is being organized. Colonel Sibley failed but his objective was a good one—from the Confederate viewpoint. Separating California from the rest of the Union by cutting the various trails would be a real victory for the South. These munitions might well be used by an invasion force."

"I doubt that guess," Baird said shortly. "I've heard other reports from Texas. The bulk of Sibley's men have gone east to support Rebel armies in Louisiana and Mississippi."

"Then there is the third idea. The arms cache is no secret in northern New Mexico. People have been gossiping about it for months. Also, this part of the country is swarming with deserters, outlaws, bounty-jumpers, draft-dodgers and a variety of eastern criminals who have been forced to come out here for one reason or another. Suppose they were to get hold of this supply of arms and ammunition? Instead of Indian raids there would be guerrilla attacks for plunder purposes."

The rain had slackened almost as swiftly as it had begun. Thunder still banged around them but now it was in the east. The storm had definitely passed over. "I'd better get out of here," Baird whispered hastily. "What's your guess? Of the three possibilities, I mean."

"The third. It sounds wildest but I have pretty good advice that the arms have been moved from where the Confederates left them. Possibly they have been stolen for this outlaw scheme."

"Any idea where they've been moved to?" he asked, beginning to push out through the break in the canvas.

"Conflicting reports," she said hastily. "The arms were supposedly left on the Pecos by the Confederate force there. Another Confederate group is supposed to have moved everything to a spot somewhere to the north, possibly on a tributary of the Red. Still another account says that the cache is now close to the Cimarron."

"Any choice of what to believe on that matter?"

"No. But it does appear that something is about to happen. Any talk of moving supplies sounds suspiciously like preparation for some kind of operation."

"I'll find some way to get in touch and hear the rest," he told her as he backed out. Ethan's voice was already being raised in a series of orders. The storm was over. It was time to make repairs and get back to business.

Baird was so intent on the information that had just been passed to him that for a moment or two he didn't realize that the canvas at the rear of the big wagon had been opened and that Mrs. Davenport was watching him come down from the ambulance seat.

Her comment was cordial—although more than a shade pointed. "It was a nice storm, wasn't it? For some people."

He gave her his best grin. "I liked it fine, ma'am." Then he slithered through the mud to where Ethan and Dirk were making certain that the rope corral was still intact. It occurred to him that he ought to keep an eye on that blonde woman. She seemed to have a lot of ideas—and he could not be sure that they were entirely personal ones. Maybe she knew more than he had suspected.

Warner broke in on his thoughts. "What d'ye think, Baird? Any good in tryin' to travel any more before night? Mud's deep."

Baird pulled a foot out with difficulty, almost losing a boot. "Teams couldn't make it," he said shortly. "Better stay here and get an early start, maybe even a couple of hours after midnight. This sand ought to shed the water pretty fast."

"Like I figgered," Warner nodded. "Did ye find out anything from the woman?"

Baird told him briefly about the munitions cache and the belief that it had been moved for some unknown purpose. There would be time later to start guessing whether the men who intended to use the arms were Rebels, outlaws, or Indians. He was glad to note that both Dirk and Luis had moved closer to listen. The time had come when he needed to confide in both of them. Perhaps one or the other of them might actually have information which would clear up some of the puzzling parts.

He put it to Luis directly. "Luis, if you were plan-

ning to attack Colorado settlers or one of the Arkansas
River forts, where would you hide your arms supply,
assuming that you could move one into position ahead
of time? In other words, if you were the one who
moved those guns from the original cache along the
Pecos, where would you hide them?"

The answer came with no hesitation at all. "Perdito
Canyon. No one goes there because few except
Indians know it is there. It is only a few miles from the
Arkansas."

Baird whistled softly. "That's summing up the evidence in a few words! Sounds like you might have it.
Could you take me there?"

There was no time for Luis to do more than nod.
At that point Mrs. Haislip appeared on the wagon
seat, shouting angrily to know why the wagons could
not move immediately to get away from this dismal
country.

"Jest jump down, ma'am," Warner shouted in reply.
"Ye'll find out."

He turned his back on her further protests to aim a
frown at Baird. "Ye'd better talk to her, Baird. I've
had about as big a bellyful of her as I'm fixin' to take.
Settle her hash somehow, will ye?"

Then he swung to bark, "Luis! Dirk! Git yer hosses
and scout a mite. If'n we're gonna stay here tonight
I don't want no midnight callers gittin' up on them
bluffs." Still in the same angry humor he plodded
across through a puddle to yell at the little man who
had driven the big wagon. "Shorty! Rustle yer stumps
and gather up some brush. Git dead stuff, if'n ye have
a choice. We'll heat up some vittles jest as soon as we
kin git the stuff to burn. Then I want fires out 'fore
dark."

Baird smiled at the Vermonter's show of brisk authority. Then he ignored Mrs. Haislip's continuing
complaints to follow the wagoner. Finding any kind
of fuel in this country would not be easy. Getting it
to burn would be even more difficult. Still, it seemed

likely that they could gather enough dry brush to make coffee.

Without any particular effort he learned that his fellow brush collector was called Eddie Dyland and that he had been employed by Colonel Haislip for many years. He had been left to take care of Mrs. Haislip when the Colonel left Fort Fillmore for the South. Now he was trying to see that she arrived home safely.

That much came without trouble. Otherwise, the little man didn't answer questions, his silence so complete that Baird couldn't quite decide what it meant. Dyland was either very stupid, or smart enough to make himself appear so. It was something which needed to be considered. Dyland might well become a source of trouble.

Chapter 8

When Dirk and Luis came in at dusk, they reported that they had made a wide sweep but had seen no trace of the ambush party. They thought that there would be no move by the enemy before at least another day.

By that time the wagon camp had become almost efficient. The two younger women were doing well with the simple camp cooking, Dyland feeding wet brush into the fire at the proper intervals. It had been a tedious chore to get the blaze started but Warner had exhibited considerable skill and vast patience. Now Dyland was doing equally well, pushing the brush into the fire soon enough for it to dry out in time to become fuel, but not so soon that too much of the precious stuff would burn at once. The little teamster seemed pretty competent—for a man who acted stupid.

After lending a hand with some of the chores, Baird managed to keep a close watch on the personal contacts in the camp by the simple device of heating some water and beginning the painful chore of scraping off some of his whiskers.

"Ground's dryin' up fast," Warner commented as he

drifted past. "Weather's warmin' up. I reckon we'd better move soon after midnight."

When Baird merely nodded, he growled, "After ye git all purtied up, which one o' them females are ye fixin' to charm?"

Baird went on with the tedious business of exposing his square chin. Out of the corner of his mouth he replied, "All of 'em."

"Good luck with the fat one."

"Don't be jealous." Then he added seriously, "I think I'll try to throw out some bait after a while. Kinda keep your eyes open and see if you spot any signs of a nibble."

"Meanin' what? If ye're expectin' any help outa me, ye'd best let me know what ye're expectin' from some-body else."

"I don't know. That's the truth. I keep thinking that these women—and likely Dyland—are Secesh. Maybe they've heard talk which meant nothing to them when they heard it. A little talk might stir up a reaction. Just watch for anything that looks like a show of surprise or particular interest. Maybe we can add up some hints and find a few answers."

He waited until Warner had explained the plan for a very early start. Then he took over, seeming to address himself chiefly to Mrs. Haislip. "Folks, I think we'd better understand each other a little better. You already know that these men of the Colorado Cavalry are undertaking an escort assignment which is not properly theirs. They'll do their best to see you through in safety but they'll need help. I should tell you now that I only happened to be in contact with them when we saw that ambush party acting suspi-ciously. I joined them because it seemed to be the proper thing to do. Now I want to tell you that I am Captain Baird, United States Army. I am on a special mission into this area for an odd reason. When I was at West Point I knew a fellow cadet named Joe Madison. There are all sorts of reports that Madison is behind some mysterious trouble in this area. My duty is to learn whether Madison is really here. I happened to be the only available man near here who could recognize him. Otherwise, I fear that I have no qualifications for doing much of anything."

Mrs. Davenport smiled happily. "Then I'll put your mind at ease. I happen to know Captain Madison. He visited my husband several times at Fort Garland. A very charming man, I might say."

"Rowena!" Mrs. Haislip snapped in obvious alarm.

"Don't worry," Baird said casually. "This is nothing to be hidden. It is all in the past—and on record. Southern officers discussed their problem a great deal before they decided what each individual would do about it. In this instance, Captain Madison elected to remain in Colorado and try his hand at recruiting a force which might help Colonel Sibley. Captain Davenport decided to go south and join Confederate forces there. The same sort of thing happened all over the country." He gave the blonde a cheerful grin as he asked, "That's a nice, fair way to sum it up, isn't it?"

"Much fairer than the way I've heard it described by others." Her tone was almost grim for a moment. Then she met his glance with some of the coquetry he had noted earlier. "I assume that you know a great deal about Captain Madison's efforts."

"Everyone in southern Colorado knows, I think. I've been hearing tales ever since I came down here from the Platte. It seems to have been no fault of Madison's that his regiment of Confederate militia never had a chance to help Sibley."

"Just what are you getting at, Captain Baird?" Mrs. Haislip demanded formally. Her tone had altered a shade but Baird couldn't quite understand the meaning of the change. Maybe she had decided that she must play a more diplomatic game or maybe it was just snobbishness betraying itself. Discovering that she was talking with a commissioned officer might have made a difference to her. "I assure you that Joseph Madison has not been in this area since last April."

"You are positive?"

"Of course. A woman in my position has sources of information. Go back to your whining Yankee generals and tell them to stop blaming things on Captain Madison!"

"Thank you." He bowed formally. "Joe Madison and I were once on very good terms. You relieve my mind when you assure me that he is not planning wholesale murder."

"Rubbish! That's just nervous Yankee imagination. Southerners do not plan mass murders."

"Some of them do, ma'am. So do some Yankees. Right now we're concerned with a plot to murder a great many Colorado settlers—including the women and children. The ambush attempt today seems to be part of that plot. And you'd better take my word for it that murder was intended. I heard the order given to wipe out this wagon outfit."

"I don't believe it!"

"You'd *better* believe it! Today, men were ordered to kill you. We think they will try again to carry out their orders. It would help us to fight them off if we knew why they want to do it."

"It certainly has nothing to do with Captain Madison," Mrs. Davenport broke in. "He really is not in the West."

"It suits me fine to have it that way. Now we need to know who wants you ladies dead."

"Simply some murderous desperadoes!" Mrs. Haislip exclaimed. "In this country there are savages of more than one color, you know."

Baird shook his head. He was stirring up quite a bit of talk but as yet he hadn't caught anything that sounded very important to him. "This particular band of desperadoes went to a lot of trouble to lay that ambush. Some of them were sent across from the Raton Mountains for the purpose. They were met here by a man who had been watching you all the way from Fort Union. It wasn't a haphazard attack and it was no mistake. They knew who they planned to kill. There must have been a strong reason for it."

"Ask Mrs. Rexford. Perhaps she knows something about it."

"I'm asking all of you."

"Well, I don't know!"

"Think hard, Mrs. Haislip. There are some mighty nasty things happening out here in this part of the country. Some of them may have the backing of the Confederate government since they would embarrass the Federal government. It seems highly possible that you have learned something which you do not consider important but which worries someone. Suppose this unknown someone is afraid you will unconsciously betray a secret. That would be a sufficient reason for murder in times like these."

"Nonsense, I tell you! I don't know about any plots or plans or anything!"

"Perhaps someone simply thinks that you know. That would be just as good a reason for worrying about you." He could see that he was getting to her but he couldn't see any real signs of weakening.

"There is simply nothing to know," she stated positively. "The Confederacy is no longer interested in this miserable country out here."

Baird grinned. "Nobody could blame them." That eased the tension enough for him to throw his bomb. "What do you know about a plan called Cimarron Thunder?"

She started to shake her head, then looked up suddenly. "You're not serious!"

"I was trying to be. Murder is not a joking matter. Do you know anything about Cimarron Thunder?"

"Enough to be somewhat amused that your Yankee friends should be worried. Cimarron Thunder was a madman's dream."

"Was?"

"Of course. Our government forbade Captain Biddleton to continue with his plans. When he continued to make preparations he was arrested."

Baird caught Pat Rexford's little nod at the menttion of the name. 'Do you care to tell me any more about it?" he asked quietly.

"Of course not."

"Then I'll tell you. Captain Biddleton had a scheme to retrieve Colonel Sibley's failure. He proposed to use arms Sibley had left behind on the Pecos. His force would be a mixture of Confederate guerrillas and renegade Indians. I can understand why the Confederate officials didn't want to be responsible for such a move—and I can understand why you don't care to talk about it."

He had watched her closely as he put his guesses together. When she didn't even look up at him he had to assume that he had assembled the pattern correctly.

Then Mrs. Davenport took over, still using the smile she had been aiming at him so often. "Cimarron Thunder is in the past, Captain Baird. It was no part of the Southern cause. I see no reason to avoid discussing it. It would have failed even if it had gotten started. You see, someone stole the arms before Biddleton recruited enough men to guard them."

Baird pulled a wry smile. "For a couple of ladies who didn't know anything dangerous, you are both doing quite well. Now go back to the point I made when we started. Someone removed that stock of arms and ammunition. Most people north of the Arkansas never even knew that such a cache of arms ever existed. I think it's pretty clear that somebody has a good reason for not wanting the facts to be known. You know those facts. So you're dangerous to our unknown plotters. That's pretty good logic, isn't it?"

"We know no more than we've told you," Mrs. Davenport told him soberly, her smile gone.

"But that's not the point. You know enough so that

you might happen to say something and get people thinking. Or maybe our mysterious plotter thinks you know more. It's not important how much you know, it's how much this unknown *thinks* you know."

He saw that he was making an impression so he kept the talk going until Warner broke it up with a reminder that there would be scant time for sleep before the wagons should be on the move. Baird managed a quick word with Pat Rexford as she started toward her own wagon. "I was doing some fancy fishing tonight. Did you see any sign of significant nibbles? Do they know anything they didn't let out?"

"I don't think so. To be honest about it, I don't think they know as much as I do. I think I'm the one these ambushers were trying to kill." She sounded steady enough as she uttered the words but Baird could sense the effort she was making to hold that steadiness.

"Any verification tonight?" he asked. "From our Reb gals, I mean?"

"A minor matter or two. Nothing important."

"Good. When starting time rolls around you're going to be ill. I'll take over the driving of your team. You can talk from behind the curtain while we travel. I think I'm beginning to understand what we're up against."

Warner called to him then, indicating that it was time to set up sentry arrangements for the night. Actually the first bit of business was for the four men to compare opinions on the evening's talk.

It took a while to thresh out the meaning of some of the questions Baird had brought up. He had to explain carefully which points were known to be facts and which were mere guesses aimed at getting some sort of reaction from the women. When all of them had it pretty well in mind, they agreed that neither of the southern women was withholding information of importance. If they knew more than they had told, they'd probably picked it up without knowing what it meant.

"Mrs. Rexford agrees with us," Baird told them then. "She seems to have a few more facts which she didn't get a chance to tell during the storm so she'll pretend to be ill when starting time rolls around. I want Warner to order me to do the driving for her. It'll give me a chance to finish our talk without it appearing that I'm making any effort to have that extra conversation."

"What the hell!" Ethan exclaimed. "How's a shaggy ole cor'pril gonna give orders to a cap'n? Which reminds me, how come ye didn't tell us ye was still an officer? Ye had me thinkin' ye was outa the army altogether."

"I told you the truth. I resigned a lieutenant's comission some years ago. Early this year I was asked to do detached service. I have been promised a captain's commission. It still hasn't caught up with me. But it's not important. I'm not an officer so far as any of you men are concerned. I mentioned it to Mrs. Haislip because she's a snob and I thought it might make her a little more willing to talk."

Luis broke in then. "I have heard many times of these guns on the Pecos. One of my cousins was on a hunting trip over there. He saw the wagons. Other people I trust have told me about them. These Texans came up the Pecos, as you have already said. They had a cannon and several wagons, some with supplies and some with guns which would be used to arm New Mexican companies Sibley expected to enlist."

"And which he didn't git," Warner grunted.

"Correct. Now this much I am sure is true. The Texans did not cache the guns on the Pecos. They had left the Pecos and had marched northward—with the wagons and with this one small cannon—when they heard about the defeat of Sibley's force in Apache Canyon. They immediately retreated to the east. I do not know why. For a time they were in camp on the

Canadian. Later they moved to Ute Fork. Again I do not know why. Finally they returned to the Rio Grande to meet Sibley's retreating army."

"Where did they leave the stuff they didn't take back with them?"

"My friends are not sure of that point. They are sure that only a few wagons went back down along the Pecos. Not as many wagons as came up. There was no cannon with the men who marched south. Most of the people who know these things believe that the material was hidden somewhere on Ute Fork."

"Where's Ute Fork?"

"Straight east from Fort Union. This seems likely because the men who hid the wagons and the guns still hoped that the attack would be made. They would leave the materials where they would be handy."

"Anything more you can tell us about this cache?"

"No more. But from a cache on Ute Fork it would be simple to move wagons north to the Cimarron. I was thinking of this when you asked before how I would do it if I had the chore of moving such weapons to a point close to the Arkansas. I think it would be quite easy to bring them to this very trail and take them on to the big river. In this past year it would have been safe. No freighters have been using the Cutoff. With a few men to handle the wagons and a few to scout for accidental prowlers, it could be done."

"There's no route across country?"

"Only dim trails. This trail is enough cross-country. For wagons and a cannon it would be much the best."

"So we may have the jackpot somewhere just ahead of us?"

"I think so. There are many men who will try very hard to make certain that we do not stumble upon their secret."

"No trouble in believing that, Luis. Some of 'em have tried pretty hard already. Next time they'll try harder."

Chapter 9

Warner cleared his throat. "Better git set fer the night. We'll be movin' early—and mebbe we'll be fightin' right soon after that."

"One thing more I'd like to hear from Luis," Baird cut in. "I wonder how he—or his cousins—feel about this talk of the cache having been raided."

"We believe it happened," Luis said quietly. "You will remember that Mrs. Haislip agreed on that."

"But who stole the stuff? And why?"

"I got a question too," Dirk interrupted. "If this gang knowed the country so good that they could pick a good hidin' place and use the easy way to git to it—how come they went to so much trouble to git Flood to join 'em? I thought we'd been takin' it fer granted that they needed him fer a guide."

"It could be a lot of things," Baird told him with a shrug. "We made one guess. It could be wrong. For all we know, Flood could have been a part of the gang all the time. He went to Denver and got mixed up in the First Cavalry so he could act as spy. When the gang got ready to make their move, they called him back."

"Then they're ready to move."

"Not necessarily. There's another possibility—and

I think it makes more sense. What if there's two gangs?"

"That is also my thought," Luis said quietly. "One party knows the country. They stole the guns and moved them. The other party does not know the country. They want to find these guns. They hire Flood to show them what he thinks is the most likely hiding place."

"Which cousin dreamed up that one?" Warner demanded sourly.

Baird chuckled dryly. "A smart cousin. I think it's the answer."

"So what does it mean to us?" Warner growled. "We ain't gonna be messin' with neither of 'em. It ain't none of our business in the fust place and we got them damned wimmen to haul north in the second place."

"It'll soon get to be our business," Baird told him. "If somebody is trying to keep Mrs. Rexford from making a report about this business, we'll be right in the middle of everything. That talk of mine tonight about the other women being the murder targets was just part of my fishing expedition. It's Mrs. Rexford who's the danger to these plotters."

"It still ain't none of our affair. We . . ."

Baird grinned in the darkness. Then he said slowly, "You are a complete fraud, Corporal Warner. You don't propose to let them get a crack at Mrs. Rexford —any more than I do. And it's my job to see her safely to Fort Larned. You'll be just as anxious as anybody to take a crack at any outlaw crowd that happens along—whether they've got Flood with them or not. So let's stop muttering and see if we can't agree on what we've got to expect. I think that the arms cache was raided first by some of those Confederate hotheads we talked about this evening. They're out to stir up an Indian uprising, either to egg the Indians into fighting alone or as allies. This is the Cimarron Thunder plan we've been hearing about. The plan is still active, even though the head lunatic has been arrested by Confederate authorities. I think they hid the stuff close to the Arkansas while they took time to recruit men—and Indians. Meanwhile a bunch of outlaws got wind of the plan, maybe because they were approached by recruiters. Some bright gentleman came up with a plan of his own. This is a good way to arm guerrillas who can raid for profit. Like Quantrill's operation in Missouri, they'll probably put on a show of acting for the Confederate government but the real idea will be to rob anybody who can be hit. They know how weak the forts are. They know that the garrisons can't even defend the posts, let alone interfere with raiders. All they need is a supply of guns and ammunition."

"I think you have worked it out," Luis said without showing any sign of emotion. "These men do not know where to search. They bring Flood into their ranks because they think he will know the best possible places. And I think that Flood knows. Perdito Canyon is perfect for their purpose—and no other place within many miles meets all of the demands of those who hid the arms there."

"Can you take us to it?"

"Whoa!" Warner interrupted. "We ain't got no call to go huntin' guns. We got all we kin handle jest gittin' these wagons through."

"That's your job," Baird told him. "You took the orders from the Fort Union officer. My job is to get Mrs. Rexford to safety. Somehow I've got a feeling that I can do it best by making a try at destroying this source of danger to everybody."

Luis nodded and Warner grunted unhappily for a few moments. Then the Vermonter asked, "How fur did ye say this place was, Luis?"

"A day and a half. Straight ahead."

"Hell! We won't have no chance o' gittin' there. Flood and his crowd will git there fust easy." The thought seemed to cheer him for he began to snap

out his orders for the night sentry duty. Dirk drew the
first watch but Baird promptly traded with him. When
a man knows he is not going to sleep because he has
a lot of thinking to do, he might as well handle a
job at the same time.

It was almost midnight when he came down from
a final tour along the bluffs to arouse Warner. The
stars were bright in a cloudless sky by that time and
the Vermonter quickly realized that several hours had
passed. "Seems like this oughta be about time fer me
to 'be turnin' the duty over to Dirk," he muttered,
" 'stead o' jest startin' my shift. How come ye stayed
out there so damned long? See somethin'?"

"Not a thing. I simply wanted to figure out a few
facts. With so many rumors it's hard to know what
to believe."

"Ain't ye satisfied with the way we worked it out
this evenin'?"

"Almost. I'll know more about it when I check with
Mrs. Rexford."

Warner chuckled in the darkness. "Keep yer mind
on yer business. I ain't so damned sure I would if'n
I had that gal fer a partner. She's about the purtiest
widder I ever seen."

"Maybe that's another reason why I want to keep
her alive. I'll tell you all about it along around midmorning."

It seemed to him that he hadn't even closed his eyes
when Luis shook him awake and passed along the
orders Warner had already issued. When he saw shadows moving about in the darkness, he realized that
the camp was up. Horses were being harnessed to
their wagons and there was a subdued murmur of
voices on all sides. Warner had let him sleep through
the opening chores, repaying him for the extra sleep
that the other men had been able to get.

They went through the moves that had been ar-
ranged. Mrs. Rexford had complained of a sick head-

ache and Warner bustled over to tell Baird that he
would have to drive the wagon. Luis and Dirk were
already moving out as an advance guard. There had
been no sign of trouble during the middle part of the
night so it seemed that all plans were working
properly.

That was when Mrs. Davenport came through the
darkness to where Baird was tying his horse to the
rear of the ambulance. A shadowy figure behind her
indicated that Warner was aware of her movements
but was going to let Baird handle the matter.

"I declare, Captain Baird," she announced in an
accent far broader than her usual speech, "I don't
think you ought to have all of this responsibility.
When a woman is ailin', she ought to have womenfolk
to help her. I'll just ride along on that wagon with
you—and be handy to take care of her if she needs
me." The tone she had adopted left him to wonder.
Was this a matter of a woman having suddenly become
attracted to a man? Or was she playing that role for
some purpose of her own? One way or another it was
not the kind of arrangement he wanted.

"Sorry, Mrs. Davenport," he told her, thinking
hard. "I don't believe we can spare you from your
other duty."

"What other duty?" she asked in evident surprise
and disappointment.

"I guess Corporal Warner didn't explain. The trail
is very poor now, few wagons using it at this time of
year. Yesterday's storm will make it harder to find—
and we're going to be moving in the blackest part of
the night. Your wagon will have to follow Corporal
Warner closely so as not to get lost. I think you
understand why we can't trust Eddie Dyland to do
that duty very well. You'll have to sit up there with
him and make sure that you never lose sight of
Warner."

The Vermonter took his cue promptly. "I was jest
comin' along to tell ye about that, ma'am," he broke

in from the deeper shadows. "And another thing—we could run into another ambush any time this mornin'. We're kinda countin' on havin' one sensible critter on that wagon if'n it comes to shootin'. Somebody's got to ride herd on a half-wit driver and a flannel-mouth ole woman."

A giggle broke through her halfhearted protest and then she slipped away in the darkness. Warner came close to Baird, whispering, "Dam' if that shave didn't git the wimmen! It don't seem real fair. Ye've got the purtiest ones in the territory. Two of 'em."

"I've got nobody. Let's get on the way before somebody else gets them—the wrong way."

By that time, Dirk and Luis had a good ten-minute start. Warner rode out ahead, calling sharp but low-voiced orders to Eddie Dyland. Then he repeated what he had told Mrs. Davenport about following him and not looking for trail ruts. The ground seemed to have dried out well during the night but there would be low patches with mud in them. Warner would decide whether to pull through them or go around. The important matter was to keep him in sight.

Baird climbed to the ambulance seat without speaking, waiting in the blackness until he saw the bulky shadow of the first wagon beginning to fade into the less distinct shadow that was the night itself. Then he slapped the reins across the backs of the horses, urging them into reluctant motion. Only then did he ask in a low voice, "How's the invalid?"

Her reply came from a point so close to his shoulder that he knew she must be sitting on that chest he had climbed over in entering and leaving the wagon during the storm. "I was almost ready to declare myself cured. But you got rid of the volunteer nurse so I'll just let myself go on worrying about the mess I'm in. I could get that headache quite easily."

"Better stop worrying and start thinking. We've got to find a way out of this. Luis told me about the arms cache last night. Suppose I tell you what we know

and what we think? Then you can try your hand at
pointing out mistakes."

He went over the facts they had discussed at their
final session of the evening, explaining in some detail
why they had reached certain conclusions. "We're depending pretty strongly on gossip supplied by New
Mexican peons. Luis thinks they really know the
truth."

"I hope they do," she murmured. "I also have used
the same sources. My husband had many friends a-
mong them. They would not lie to me."

There was a brief silence before she continued, "Let
me explain my part in all this. Then perhaps you'll
be able to judge the value of the information I am
carrying. Before I married and came to Santa Fe with
my husband I worked for the War Department as a
code clerk, a cryptography expert really—if you don't
mind my sounding a trifle boastful. I had simply
turned a childhood hobby into a useful occupation.
Anyway, when friends back East heard of my husband's death, they suggested to my former chief that
I should return to the War Office. With so many
messages being intercepted, so much Confederate
espionage haunting the capital, it would seem that the
government needs all the help it can get in the code
department."

"Hold up," he interrupted, pulling on the reins as
he saw the shadow ahead looming blacker. "We're
closing in on the other wagon."

They were silent while he followed the larger vehicle across a shallow gully where mud caused only
minor difficulty. Then he opened up the interval and
said, "Go on. You're on your way back to Washington."

"Not quite. Before I even decided to accept the
offer, I was approached by a gentleman in Santa Fe
whose name you would probably recognize if I were to
mention it. He told me that he was serving as an
agent of the United States, working secretly to guard

against the treason which was known to exist in so
many places. He asked me to use my contacts with
the ordinary people of the territory to investigate
certain reports of treachery." Her voice altered slightly
as she added, "Poor people know a great deal, espe-
cially in a society like that of New Mexico where a
feudal vestige still exists. The peon is just a part of
the scenery to important people. Peons are ignored,
almost forgotten. They thus become excellent intelli-
gence agents because they are practically unseen ob-
servers. The trouble is that they have learned through
generations of harsh experience that it is not safe to
admit that they know so many things. Officials cannot
get it out of them, even when the New Mexican has
become part of a Federal military unit. It was believed
that I could do something. These people trusted me
as they trusted my husband."

"Señora Rey," Baird murmured. "I think I understand. I also begin to think more of Luis and his
cousins, the ones who seem to know so much."

"That is good," she told him out of the darkness.
"I am sure that some of those cousins are also my
sources of information. I know of Luis. He is all
right."

"What did you learn?"

"Much of treason. It shocked me, of course. It
shocked me still more when I reported to the man who
had set me to the task and he told me that I must
not make any official report to either the civil or
military authorities because they would either bury
the report—or try to bury me."

"Somebody's still trying," Baird told her grimly.

"Not the authorities now. Someone else."

"Then you have an idea what that ambush meant?"

"I do. First, let me say that I believe your information and your assumptions are quite sound. You
are even ahead of me with regard to the part about the
moving of those Pecos munitions. All I could learn
was that they had been moved from the original cache

on Ute Fork. I think it was Captain Biddleton's men who moved them, the men who call themselves the Pecos Volunteers. It is indeed their program which is known as Cimarron Thunder. Mrs. Haislip was quite honest about it last evening. It is a madman's scheme, disavowed by Confederate officials. However, it is not dead. The fanatics who were drawn to Biddleton in the first place are still fanatics. They intend to carry out his idiocy even though he may be a prisoner somewhere in Texas. They want to create so much fear in Colorado and Kansas that the federal government will have to weaken its attack on the Confederacy by diverting troops to this area."

"Are these men guarding the new cache?"

"I do not know. No one around Santa Fe or Fort Union even knew where the new hiding place might be. The general belief was that the arms had been removed and hidden while the leaderless followers find some new men, possibly Indians."

"Now what about the other gang? Do you suppose they are what we guessed, hijackers with a plan to plunder?"

"I am sure of it. I can even name the brains behind the scheme. Because I can name him he cannot afford to let me get through to loyal officials who can order his arrest. I have no doubt whatever that he ordered the ambush."

"Now we're getting somewhere. Who is he?"

"A government contractor who makes his headquarters at Fort Union. His name is Hickey, Martin Hickey. He has had government contracts of all types for years but has gained influence far beyond what you'd expect a freight contractor to have. To put it bluntly, he is the criminal brain of northern New Mexico. Many people think he is a loyal Unionist because he provided many wagons and teamsters to move the First Colorado into Apache Canyon where they halted Sibley's force. I am sure Hickey's motive was something less than patriotic. He simply did not want anything interfering with the profitable arrangements he had made with grafting Union officers."

"He is the one who plans to steal the Cimarron Thunder arms?"

"Yes. It is too big an operation for him to ignore. The profits would be huge. He might even find himself in control of a large part of the west. In one sense, he is almost as great a fanatic as Biddleton except that his motive is different. He wants power and wealth for himself while Biddleton is patriotic in his own crazy fashion."

"He suspects that you have gotten onto him?"

"I think so. A man I know to be a Hickey lieutenant passed our wagons the first day out of Fort Union. I think he was making certain that I was moving up the Cimarron Trail. I also think he must be the man who met the ambushers just before we arrived. You mentioned such a man."

"But Hickey had it planned earlier, I imagine," Baird commented. "When he ordered his outlaws across from the Ratons it seems pretty evident that they had two lots of orders. They brought Flood—to help them find the cached guns—but they halted along the trail and were ready to do their bushwhacking. I'm afraid you're important enough to this Hickey for him to have gone to considerable trouble to murder you."

Again her voice altered just a little. "Isn't it odd the way we discuss these things in such matter-of-fact style? A year ago I wouldn't have believed that I could even think about it without becoming a screaming wreck."

"Keep thinking the way you're doing," he advised. "It'll help."

Shortly after daybreak they had to make a rather difficult crossing of a gully which was still in flood from the storm. It took considerable effort to get the wagons across but there was one good feature. The water was running quite clear and Warner saw to it that the horses drank what they wanted.

"With a bit of luck we'll git through to the Arkansas on what's in the barrels now," he told Baird. "I'm kinda lookin' forward to seein' that damned river. When we hit the other trail we got a chance o' meetin' friends."

"Don't get to thinking too far ahead. Long before we reach the Arkansas we've got a much better chance of meeting enemies." He reported the talk he had exchanged with Pat Rexford.

Warner scratched his whiskers ruefully. "Looks like we got ourselves a purty dam' mess. Biddleton's lunatics are out here somewhere, mebbe with more idiots to help 'em out. This Hickey's got one crowd we know about all ready to shoot us full o' holes. Mebbe there's more. I'd kinda figger it's gonna take more'n a few barrels o' water to git us to the Arkansas."

Dirk came in then, reporting that there was dry country ahead. The storm had been as limited in range as most such storms were. Also there was no sign of the bushwhackers. Either they were still at the hideout in the hills or they were avoiding the trail as they rode forward to some new ambush spot.

"We'll stop right here," Warner decided suddenly. "Teams need a rest. We'll have a bite o' grub while there's brush around fer fires. Pass the word. Dirk, ye'd better eat here, then send Luis in."

Chapter 10

When the wagons were ready to roll again, Mrs.
Rexford put in an appearance, declaring herself fully
recovered and ready to handle the reins. Baird accordingly took over the duty of covering the rear. Now
that it was light and the wagons could be seen by
distant watchers, it would be important to have all
flanks covered.

They moved with the exasperating slowness of
heavy wagons on sandy soil, everyone aware of the
need for haste but Warner battling Mrs. Haislip's
urgency. He didn't propose to let her force the pace
to the extent that there would be danger of exhausting
the teams.

At midday Luis dropped back as though to make
some sort of report. Baird saw the move and closed in
on the wagons after making certain that there was no
enemy on the rear flanks. Before he could talk to
the New Mexican, he saw that there were two women
now on the seat of the ambulance. He swung by and
asked, "Are you feeling worse again, Mrs. Rexford?"
He made it sound serious, almost worried.

The blonde woman gestured impatiently. "I'm the
one who's feeling ill. After days in that wagon with
Margaretta Haislip, anyone would get sick!"

"I guess she gets to be a real earache after a while," Baird conceded in a low voice. "Does she try to order you around all the time like she does with the rest of us?"

"That's the entire problem. She has been the wife of a post commander for so many years that she has become a petty tyrant. And I stood it because I had let myself become the perfect junior officer's wife! You men showed me that she doesn't have to be treated the way she wants to be!"

Baird didn't bother to swap glances with Pat Rexford. He knew exactly what she was thinking—and he agreed. Mrs. Davenport was determined to keep an eye on matters involving the second wagon. Whether her interest was personal or political really didn't matter much. The whole affair was reaching the stage where everything had to come out into the open.

"That's the way to talk," he told her with a smile. "If you don't like the company you're keeping— secede!" Then he rode on to meet Luis and Ethan.

"Still no sign of the enemy," Luis told him. "I think we should decide on the amount of distance we must cover today. There is scrub timber country not many miles ahead of us. Also we are getting closer to the approach to Perdito Canyon."

He spelled it out for them as they rode together ahead of the wagons. Timing would be important. The wagons had made slow progress in spite of the early start. Nightfall would find them close to the timber. A second ambush had to be expected where there was cover for the ambushers.

"If we camp well short of this brush country," he explained, "I think we will not be attacked during the night, since they will prefer to try another bush-whacking plan. However, if we must cover much open country tomorrow before entering the timber, they will have more time to prepare. Also, we may have to fight our way through. Perhaps we could not do that in the daylight of one day. If we are still in the brush at nightfall, we would be at their mercy."

"You've got a plan?" Baird asked shortly.

"A poor one, I'm afraid. I think we should make camp in the middle of the afternoon. They will see us, of course. As soon as it becomes fully dark we move again, this time to the edge of the brush country. At dawn we make our real move and get ready for the fight. It is the only way, I fear. At least we will have the full day to make our way through to more open country."

Baird nodded. "You're the one who knows the country. You'll have to decide on the strategy."

"Then we try to fight them?"

"What choice do we have? We can't stay here."

Warner interrupted to ask, "Where do ye figger Flood and the rest of 'em is at by this time? Ain't there been no sign yet?"

"No sign yet. But they will head into the timber, I am sure. Flood will see to that. He knows that it gives them ambush chances, also that it makes the best approach to Perdito Canyon."

"Which is off to our right now?" Baird asked.

"To the right and ahead."

They saw Dirk galloping back toward them then and Warner swore irately. "What the hell kind o' scouts have we got in this tinhorn army? Nobody out there watchin' nothin'!"

Luis swung wide to ride a slight rise of ground. He was obviously looking for signs of pursuit behind Dirk but after a few minutes he came back to the others, holding his peace while Warner continued to sputter.

Finally Dirk was close enough to shout, "They're ahead of us, Ethan. Tracks crossed the main trail. Five riders. No extry ponies."

"They didn't continue on the trail?" Baird asked.

"Nope. Cut across and headed east."

Luis shook his head. "I do not like it. They ride from the hills and toward the canyon."

"What the hell's wrong with that?" Warner demanded. "We don't care where they're goin' if they're not movin' into position ahead of us."

"But they are. This is a trick. They want us to think that they no longer are interested in us. They will circle back to the Cutoff trail and make their ambush preparations in the timber."

"Mebbe not. If'n Flood is anxious to find this Perdito Canyon place, he could be willin' to fergit about us."

"I do not think so. They have their orders about Mrs. Rexford. Possibly there is already a dispute between those who want to carry out the orders and those who wish to seize the guns. But I try to think as I believe Flood will think. If he has decided that the guns are hidden in Perdito Canyon, he will also believe that I have reached the same conclusion. It is now important that all of us be wiped out."

"Sounds likely," Baird agreed.

"And for yet another reason. I believe that the fine scheme of this man Hickey is not yet ready to start operating. The sufficient number of men is not yet on hand. A few men may seize the hidden guns but it will require many more to make use of them. Capturing the guns is not enough; they must keep everything secret until they are ready to move."

"I'm convinced," Baird said simply. "Mrs. Rexford is not the only one who can get word sent east about the plot. They don't want it to leak."

He turned to the hulking blond youth. "Dirk, swap jobs with me, will you? Get back there and cover the rear. I want to ride ahead with Luis and look things over. Maybe we can find some way out of this nutcracker."

"Why not try to move up in a hurry?" Warner proposed. "If they're waitin' fer more men it'll be a good move to start tradin' lead with 'em while the odds ain't so bad."

Baird chuckled with grim humor. "Ethan, you keep forgetting. This is not your trouble, remember? Don't be so anxious to start a fight."

He spurred the chestnut forward before Warner could find a reply. Luis overtook him moments later and they were a quarter of a mile ahead of the wagons when they stopped to examine the tracks Dirk had reported.

"Five of 'em, all right," Baird muttered. "Seven men at the start. One dead in the first ambush, one wounded. I suppose they've left the wounded man behind."

"Perhaps for a reason. They were at a known hangout. It is possible that the wounded man remained behind to tell expected reinforcements where they should go. It seems very clear that such additional outlaw forces are expected."

Baird studied the gently rolling barrens ahead. "More outlaws. We figured it that way, all right. In this country they won't try anything. It's too open. So let's have a look at that trail. We won't go wide enough but what we can get back to the wagons if anything starts."

"It is not necessary, I think," Luis said quietly. "Again I try to think as Sergeant Flood would think. In his place I would leave a false trail in a wide but narrow loop to the right of the Cutoff. I would expect that simple Luis to follow it because he would think it meant a move toward Perdito Canyon. I would not expect him to follow it very far because such a move would leave the wagons without protection. So I would double back when I had reached a point which I would not expect him to reach. That would leave the proper impression on the mind of this simple peon."

Baird chuckled. "Is it possible that Sergeant Flood was not with you fellows long enough to discover that Luis Martinez is not the simple peon he pretends to be?"

"I am hoping that it is so." Luis was being very serious now but it was quite clear that he was pleased by Baird's remark. "I think we should ride as flankers but far out beyond the usual distance. In that way we have a better chance to spot ambushers before they see us. They will be watching the trail, not the arroyos at a distance from it."

"Then you're sure they're setting up a new ambush?"

Luis shrugged. "What else?"

"I agree. So I'll take the wide swing on the right. I'm curious to see how soon I cut the trail of the men coming back to fool poor simple Luis Martinez. You handle the left. It's just possible that they may have swung to that side because they'll hope we'll be looking for them on the right."

"It is a good thought," Luis told him, still keeping to the pose of grave dignity. "Be very alert at a distance of about one mile. Many arroyos are in that area. I think the ambushers will use one of them to make their return from the false trail."

Baird gave him a salute which matched the tone. "I heed the advice of one who thinks well and has many intelligent cousins." Then they exchanged grins and separated. It was only when he was well to the southeast that Baird remembered something. They had not made any actual agreement about halting the train short of the brush country. He hoped Warner would use his head.

The thought brought back the tension which had been briefly eased by his exchange with Luis. He warned himself grimly that this was no time to be making even simple mistakes. Warner would probably make the halt they had discussed but the matter should not have been left to chance. With danger in every direction there was no point in taking even the tiniest extra risk.

The thought made him move with added care as he

swung wide on the scouting chore. But he could still let his mind run over the guesses they had been making, checking mentally to see how close the guesses were coming to verification. He knew that he had to anticipate at least two parties of enemies ahead. Every bit of information pointed that way. The party of immediate concern had to be a part of Hickey's outlaw band. They were the ones who had found it necessary to recruit Jeremiah Flood because none of them knew this Cimarron country. They were the ones who had received orders to murder Pat Rexford. They were the ones who had been ready to massacre an entire wagon party to get Mrs. Rexford. They were the ones who had previously ambushed and murdered a part of Sergeant Flood's patrol—with Flood's connivance.

"Adds up real nice," Baird said half aloud. "Expect the worst from 'em. That's the way they work."

He didn't forget that the other party might be just as ruthless. They were the men who had moved the guns from the Pecos. Perhaps they were now standing guard over the cache—on Perdito Canyon or elsewhere. More likely they had left a guard while the rest of the company went on a recruiting tour. Some of them were very likely recruiting renegade Indians. Expecting anything but savagery from this crowd was just as irresponsible as it could be.

By the time he was ready to make his swing into a line roughly parallel to the wagon trail, he had ridden completely away from all signs of the recent storm. The ground was not even damp in this part of the wasteland. It made him realize once more why wagons avoided the Cimarron Trail at this time of year. Even the arduous climb across Raton Pass would be preferable to this desert journey.

He had been keeping watch behind him as he made his swing out from the wagon trace, turning only when Luis had disappeared and the wagons were tiny specks in the distance. Now he should be far enough away to avoid detection by sentinels ahead. If men were watching the approaching wagons, they would not be doing much looking in his direction.

Within a half mile after making his turn, he began to see the broken country Luis had mentioned. The land seemed to slope a little to his right and he guessed that these arroyos would drain into Perdito Canyon when they became streams in the rainy season. It was not really important. What *was* important was the fresh sign he found in the second arroyo. Five riders had traveled through the little gulley toward the Cimarron Trail. Luis had called the shot exactly.

He made a careful study of the surrounding region before taking up the trail of the five riders. Ahead and to his right there were several patches of green against the background of dull yellows and browns. This would be the outer fringes of the brush country Luis had mentioned. Ambush country. Where there was vegetation there was cover. Ambushers would use it to their advantage. It was exactly what he had known must be expected but realization came grimly just the same. Danger ahead in the distance was one thing. Danger at hand was something else.

The trail he followed broke away out of the arroyo here. The outlaws seemed to be heading toward one of the green patches, but Baird had no intention of following. He simply continued in the winding arroyo, taking an observation from time to time but concentrating on remaining out of sight.

He knew that he was working back toward the wagon trail but he guessed that the flanking movement didn't need to be carried on much longer. He already knew where the enemy had gone. Their intentions could be guessed without too much trouble. Yet he kept to the hollows, working his way from one winding gulley to another.

After a few minutes he began to find higher grass and clumps of brush along the wash he was following, so he judged that he was edging into one of those outflung fingers of the scrub timber belt. He found a place where willows struggled for a precarious existence and halted for another observation. This time he saw the man who rode directly ahead of him, actually using the same arroyo for keeping out of sight. The fellow wore a blue army shirt and dark trousers which might well be of government origin. At this distance Baird could not be certain, but it didn't matter. The man was moving toward the wagon trail, using the best available cover to get into a position which would let him observe the wagons as they came up the Cimarron Trail.

A careful study of the country in all directions indicated that the man was quite alone. No attack was being organized. This fellow was probably a scout sent back to see what the wagon outfit was like. Probably the ambushers still didn't know whether the New Mexican militia still was acting as an escort. Perhaps they hadn't yet found out the strength of the party that had broken up the ambush.

Baird found himself outguessing the enemy's leader. The man who was giving the orders would have to be figuring hard. Perhaps he merely wanted to gain delay while waiting for expected reinforcements. With a party of five they would not be attempting any real attack against well-guarded wagons. However, when the truth became evident they might make the effort. With even odds the advantage would be with the ambusher.

It occurred to him that he might buy a little time by capturing the outlaw scout, but then he wondered. If the enemy also wanted delay—which he assumed but did not actually know—then he would be betting into their strength.

It also came to his mind that the man he followed might not be one of the ambush party. He could be some harmless wanderer who had no part in this tangle. That idea was discarded promptly. Harmless wanderers didn't come into this dreary country—and they didn't ride so furtively. This fellow knew that he had to keep out of sight. He knew what was ahead.

When the arroyo petered out, Baird worked his way a little to the right so as to put a sandy ridge between himself and the man he was trailing. A second ridge served to screen him from the enemy he assumed to be hiding in the first big patch of brush. Twice he paused to take observations from the side of the ridge. Each time he felt sure that he had not been seen by the bushwhackers who must now be somewhere behind him. And he was getting closer to the enemy scout, obviously with the man unaware of his presence.

Finally the fellow ducked into another of those forlorn clumps of willow, leaving his horse there while he worked his way through light brush toward a break in the same ridge Baird had been using. Obviously he intended to make this his observation post. From it he would be able to discover the pitiful weakness of the wagon outfit. Baird knew that he could not afford to let the man make his report.

Chapter 11

It took some careful stalking—and a painfully long period of time—but Baird finally managed to get into position. He left his own horse near that of the outlaw scout and inched forward, using every break in the terrain to screen his moves. Finally he was directly behind the man, a dozen yards short of the spot where the fellow lay belly down on a little dune where he could study the Cutoff Trail. The watcher was so intent on what he was seeing that he had no inkling of Baird's appraoch until it was too late for him to grab the carbine which he had placed on the ground at his side.

"Don't move!" Baird ordered. "You'll never lay a hand on that gun!"

The fellow jerked in astonishment but then froze. He didn't even try to look around. Baird barked another order. "Roll over—to the left. Not toward the gun. Go ahead. Roll again! That's fine. You roll real good. Now stay face down and get both hands up beyond your head. I'm going to lift that gun in your belt—and I'll blow a hole in the middle of your back if you even twitch!" He had gotten a good look at the rather youthful but heavily bearded face as the outlaw made his first roll. The fellow was scared and Baird intended to keep him scared.

He retrieved the carbine and a clumsy sort of revolver which was completely strange to him. Then he left the man prone and inched to a higher position that would let him get a good look at the brush area. Taking a prisoner was one thing; being captured with a prisoner was something else.

"Get up!" he ordered, still using the same harsh tone. "Walk slowly back to your horse. Careful now. I'm not at all sure I want you alive but I'll keep thinking I do unless you make the wrong move."

He herded his prisoner back toward the horses, making no real effort to stay behind cover. If the other bushwhackers were watching, they would soon know that their scout had been captured.

He mounted swiftly and held a steady gun on target while the other man climbed into his saddle. "Get going! Slow. Toward those wagons. You were so damned interested in 'em that we'll give you a good chance for a close look."

More orders snapped out as he followed. It seemed like a good idea to keep reminding his man of what would happen if he made any attempt to bolt. The flow of commands also gave Baird a chance to sneak a few looks in the direction of the first bits of heavy brush. At the second glance he saw signs of movement and wondered whether there would be pursuit. After that, however, he could detect no sign of the enemy.

Minutes later he ordered the captive to a halt beside the wagon trail. Both Warner and Luis were closing in rapidly, each of them having observed Baird's approach. Warner arrived first and Baird greeted him with a show of casual humor. "We've got company, Corporal. This bright young feller was so keen on finding out about those wagons that it seemed like a real charitable idea to let him have a close look. Too bad you stopped 'em back there, but now maybe he'd like to tell us why he was interested before we give him his close look."

Warner nodded, taking his cue from Baird's manner. "He might be real smart to do his talkin' now. If'n we have to turn him over to Dirk—" He shook his head worriedly and added, "That boy ain't had no chance to try out his muscles fer quite a spell. He could git real mean. How much did the bastard tell ye up to now?"

"Not a word. He doesn't seem to be much of a talker."

"Dirk'll fix that—quick and mebbe kinda painful."

Luis drew rein beside them then and Baird repeated what he had told Warner. The New Mexican didn't reply but simply stared hard at the silent prisoner, then at the horse. Finally he murmured, "Horse thief. And a deserter. He's wearing some of his uniform and the horse carried the government brand. I think he is in trouble."

Baird picked up the hint. "Desertion and horse stealing. That's a mighty bad combination when you think about it. They shoot deserters and hang horse thieves. Maybe they'll give this jigger a choice."

"Ah didn't steal that hoss," the prisoner exclaimed, his opening words identifying him quickly as of southern origin. "They had him and let me use him."

"Who's they?"

The youthful features took on an air of shrewdness in spite of the obvious panic. "What does it git me if'n Ah tell yo'?"

Baird shook his head. "Not a damned thing. We know all we need to know. When Dirk gets finished we'll likely know more—but it won't be important to us." He stared thoughtfully at the prisoner and went on in a less severe tone, "I could even sympathize with a young fellow like you. I suppose you got mixed up in this dirty business by accident. You found that you couldn't resign and go south like the officers did— so you deserted. Maybe you even started out with what you thought were patriotic ideas about joining state troops back home. But somehow you got mixed up with these outlaw guerrillas and now you're a criminal. It's too bad." He sounded almost sorry.

The prisoner's reaction showed something like spirit for the first time. "I ain't no hoss thief and I ain't no outlaw!" he declared. "Mebbe a deserter but yo' already told about how it happened. Now Ah'm Private Edward Laniard, Second Regiment, Pecos Volunteers. That makes me a prisoner o' wah, Ah reckon. Seems as how Ah oughta git treated that way."

Baird and the others exchanged quick glances. Pecos Volunteers. This wasn't the way they had figured it out.

Dirk had been with them long enough to have heard the last exchange and now he broke in angrily, "Ain't no use lettin' him lie about it. What I want to know is where at is that bastard Flood. Either he tells me easy or I beat it outa him!"

The boy tried hard to sound calm as he asked, "Who's Flood? Ah nevah heard of him."

"Stop playing games!" Baird snapped. "We broke up that other ambush. We know you were in it. You planned murder, pure and simple. We heard the orders to wipe out the whole wagon party. That's murder. You were a part of it. So don't try that prisoner-of-war nonsense on us!"

"Act of war," the prisoner insisted.

"You're not a Confederate unit. You were attacking civilians as well as New Mexico militia. You'd better get smart and tell us who gave those orders. You won't get any mercy otherwise. These men are friends of the party you massacred west of Two Butte Creek."

"Lemme work on him," Dirk suggested, edging forward. "He'll talk to me or he'll never talk to nobody else!"

The prisoner broke. "It was Sergeant Oakes what give the order. Him as useta be at Fort Garland with me. We deserted together when the officers was pullin' out."

"Go on," Baird prodded. "Where did you go—instead of heading South like the officers?"

"We was supposed to jine up with a officer name of Madison. He was raisin' a regiment somewhere north of Fort Garland. Somehow we never caught up with him. We kinda been on the run since then."

"You mean you've been raiding in the Ratons. Right?"

"It was war. We hit Union wagons."

"For plunder. The Confederacy claims that they have no troops in this territory. You know what that makes you. Now get on with it before Dirk has to stir you up a bit."

"Ain't much to tell. After some of us had been hidin' out in the Ratons fer quite a spell, Sergeant Oakes showed up. He left us way back in April, I think it was. He tole us that we could fergit the Madison regiment, that we belonged to a new one that was bein' raised, the Second Pecos Volunteers. Then a man named Billings showed up right behind Oakes. His message was that we should ride across to the Cimarron and pick up some guns what the Confederate gov'ment had sent up fer us. I dunno what we was supposed to do with them guns."

Baird nodded. "I think you have a pretty good idea but don't worry. We'll tell you. You were to use the guns to raid the posts and settlements along the Arkansas. Maybe you didn't even know that Oakes and Billings were lying to you. Your crowd was no part of the Pecos Volunteers. You were out to steal the guns they had cached. Then you'd use them for plunder purposes. Son, you're an outlaw, whether you know it or not!"

"Hell, he knows it!" Warner said disgustedly. "When he took orders to murder wimmen he had to know it!"

"Not wimmen!" the prisoner protested. "Jest one woman. And she is a Union spy."

Baird shook his head. "Son, either you're a bad liar or damned stupid. You're not with a Confederate force. You're with outlaws."

"But we got orders direct from Joe Johnston. Sergeant Oakes told me so!"

"Sergeant Oakes is the liar—if you're not. Joe Johnston hasn't been giving any orders to anybody since he was wounded last year in front of Richmond. I doubt if he even knows that this part of the country is out here."

He glanced at Warner. "We'd better let Luis continue a patrol here. He knows where the rest of the bushwhackers are holed up but we'll need to know if they make a move. Meanwhile Dirk can take this pilgrim back toward the wagons and let him see the women he was trying to murder."

"Tie him up," Warner added, speaking to Dirk. "Ye don't need to git gentle about it neither."

Baird waited until Dirk had taken the prisoner away, then he said in a low voice, "We'll stick just a little behind them. I'm curious to see how Mrs. Davenport and this kid are going to act when they see each other. Fort Garland is not a post of any size. If they were both there just before the war started, they ought to recognize each other."

"Ye think they both told the truth?"

"Maybe. I think the prisoner did. I'm not so sure about that blonde. She has been getting just a mite too sociable."

Warner grinned. "Depends on what ye mean by sociable. Seems like it could git interestin'."

"Likely so. I have a strong suspicion that she's not much disturbed over her husband's absence. Which maybe is a good thing. She may be a widow by this time."

Warner's chuckle came hoarsely as they started to follow the prisoner to the wagon camp. "Mebbe that's what yer waitin' fer. Seems like widders kinda appeal to ye."

"Better keep your mind on business. We're still in a mess."

"And I don't figger as how watchin' the blonde gal and this fool prisoner is gonna git us out of it. Looks to me like we jest got to bust right in on them other varmints and fight 'em off. The odds are kinda evened up."

"I'm thinking the same way. So I'd like to know everything worth knowing before we make the attempt. What bothers me most is the chance that the bushwhackers might get help too soon. Maybe we can find out something if we get these two together just right."

It didn't take but a moment to settle one point. Neither the prisoner nor Rowena Davenport made any attempt to hide mutual recognition. There was a confused exchange of half-finished questions—without answers—and then Mrs. Davenport turned to stare questioningly up at Baird. "Is this one of the men who tried to murder us yesterday, Captain Baird?"

Dirk clamped a big hand over the prisoner's mouth as he tried to say something. Baird nodded gravely. "He doesn't deny being in that bushwhack party. Do you know him?"

"Yes. He was Private Edward Laniard when he was in the garrison at Fort Garland. My husband looked upon him as a good soldier."

"He deserted."

"So did my husband, in one sense. So did many others. I don't think there is any point in our discussing the matter. We wouldn't agree. Nor is it important to us at the moment."

She was serious now, not trying any of the coy glances which she had used earlier. Baird decided that she was beginning to realize that she didn't quite understand the gravity of her own situation. "Would this man have any reason to kill either of you ladies?" he inquired.

"Of course not!"

"Let him talk, Dirk. Maybe he can tell her why he wanted to."

The prisoner's protests became so frantic that it was impossible to doubt his sincerity. He repeated what he had told them earlier but now he was clearly trying to get Mrs. Davenport to believe in his honest intentions.

Surprisingly, it was Mrs. Haislip who broke in on the excited protestations. "You are a fool, Private Laniard!" she snapped in her best martinet manner. "You have been duped. You have consorted with outlaws, not with Confederate patriots. They have lied to you."

"He's still a killer!" Dirk glowered. "He helped murder four of our boys over on Muddy Crick!"

"I wasn't even there!" Laniard shouted desperately. "I heard about it from Oakes but he tole me there was a brush with a Federal patrol."

Baird came at him again. "Was that when he told you that you were going to murder a woman spy? Which one of these women were you supposed to kill? Which one is the spy?"

"I dunno. He didn't tell me."

Mrs. Haislip grunted in disgust. "This is sheer nonsense. I insist that we stop wasting time and get these wagons moving."

"We'll be making camp right here," Baird told her without ceremony. "Get supper over early. Then I want to talk with the whole company. You should know what we're planning to do." He used the plural even though he had not discussed his idea even with Warner.

"But we still have several hours of daylight," Mrs. Haislip protested. "You say that only a small group of outlaws bar our passage. I say fight it out with them!"

Baird grinned thinly. "Sounds like Colonel Haislip speaking. But I'm sure the colonel would consider a couple of points. Our horses have covered a lot of muddy miles since very early this morning. If we get into a running fight, they'll be no good to us. Also there is a matter of geography. Moving ahead now would put us in a timber area at dusk. None of us want to be in that kind of a trap for the night."

He kneed his horse into motion and left her standing there while he rode on to where Pat Rexford waited. "You hear all of that?" he asked.

"Enough. You seem to be whittling the odds."

"A little. Have you ever heard of a Sergeant Oakes and a man named Billings?"

"Of course. Didn't I mention either name? They're Hickey's main lieutenants."

"And they're trying to make themselves sound like Biddleton's lieutenants. My guess is that they're recruiting Secesh boys like this one we captured. Not that it matters very much. We've got to fight our way through, whoever is ahead of us. All that counts is that they'll be shooting at us. We don't need to care why they're shooting."

"You really have some sort of plan?"

"Not really. We just push ahead. We have no choice."

"I'm sorry," she said in a low voice. "I'm sorry I had to get you mixed up in such a dirty business."

"Not your fault. The dirty business was here. I drew the job of finding out about it—and meeting a messenger who might tell me a few facts. I didn't know whether that messenger would turn out to be a cock-eyed leper with a beard full of cockroaches or—I'm lucky, I guess."

She smiled briefly. "That is very much a left-handed compliment, I think. But thanks anyway. I'll try to do what I can to help."

"Fine. Now let's talk to the others. They've gathered for what will have to pass as a meal. I'll tell them that my bull-headed plan is no plan at all."

Before he could have his say, however, Mrs. Davenport claimed his attention. She had been in rather close conversation with the prisoner. Laniard had told her a few things. He was scared, perhaps a little angry at the lies which had been told. At least, that was the blonde's story.

"There are only four men now waiting for us," she told Baird. "The one named Flood doesn't even want to waste time with an ambush. He has tried to persuade the others to go straight for that munitions cache —which is now not far away. Sergeant Oakes—who was in my husband's company at Fort Garland—agrees with him. The one named Billings insists on carrying out the orders to kill a spy. He knows that the proposed victim is a woman who used to live in Santa Fe. He doesn't know anything more about her. I do not know who gave him the order but he is very much afraid to fail. Does that help us any?"

"And the fourth man?"

"Private Laniard is not sure about him—but he is not one of the important ones."

"Thanks," Baird told her casually. "We'll keep it in mind. Now let's get down to business. Whether those ambushers decide one way or another it seems that we have to make our break without delay. We can't risk it tonight but we ought to move before daybreak tomorrow morning. We'll try to time the move so as to hit the brush country just as full daylight comes along. We'll have flankers out, of course, only nobody will be far from the wagons. There's a pretty good chance that they won't try to hit us when they know we're ready—and when they don't have any advantage in numbers." He grinned wryly as he added, "They didn't show any great amount of nerve when we broke up that other ambush attempt—and they had the odds on their side.

"Tomorrow we'll have something else working for us. We'll have a hostage. We'll put Laniard on one of the horses that will be hauling the first wagon. He'll be tied there—in full view. It may help to convince them that Flood is right, that there's too much risk for an attack to be worth the effort."

There were protests, but in general the idea seemed

to be getting quick acceptance. Baird started to set up detailed assignments but was interrupted when Luis came in with a report. Ten men had ridden down the trail from the northeast. They had been met at the edge of the brush country by a rider who looked like Flood. Then they had followed the supposed Flood into the timber.

"It wasn't a very good idea anyway," Baird grunted. "With fourteen instead of four—forget it!"

Chapter 12

Baird decided that his attempt at wry humor had not met with any great success. Mrs. Haislip promptly went back to being her old self, condemning Yankee blundering for the whole mess and bemoaning the fact that she had been forced to travel with a dangerous spy. Mrs. Davenport hurried across to talk frantically to the still bound prisoner. Most of the others simply swore under their breaths. Only Dyland sat and stared, maintaining the calm of the unintelligent.

"There's still light," Baird said briskly. "Luis, I'd like to see where these new outlaws disappeared. Maybe we can figure out a way to get around them." The final statement was strictly for morale purposes. He had a plan in mind, a plan which he had been working on for hours, completely hopeless as it seemed.

"I'll come along," Warner grumbled. "Dirk kin keep an eye on things—like prisoners—here in camp."

As soon as they were clear of the wagons, Baird asked, "Luis, how good are you at finding your way in the dark? Can you take me to Perdito Canyon to-night?"

"It is possible. The distance is no more than ten or twelve miles. It depends on what part of the canyon must be reached."

"Good. I've been trying to think something out. Flood wanted to go right on and grab the guns. Billings wanted to stay here and carry out his orders to kill Mrs. Rexford. They've got enough men now so that they can do both. My job is to keep them from doing either. I don't think they'll split up for the chore until morning. By that time I want to be there."

"Why?" Warner demanded. "Ye'll only git yerself boxed in between the gang what's guardin' the stuff and this other crowd what's fixin' to take it."

"It won't be any worse than trying to run that gauntlet ahead. Luis, can you find that cache in the dark?"

"Maybe. If it's where I think it is."

"Dammit!" Warner spluttered. "If I didn't have them stoopid wimmen on my neck, we'd all go. Then mebbe we'd have a chance."

Baird pulled a crooked grin. "I've just been wondering if we couldn't arrange it. With a little of the right kind of irritation maybe we could persuade Mrs. Haislip to chase us away. We're dangerous. We draw enemies."

"Ye think she might git ornery enough fer that?"

"Maybe. We've just got to remember that we can't simply abandon the two of them. The authorities sent them east under guard for their own protection. At the moment you are the official protector. If anything happens to either of them, there will be a very large stink. A lot of folks who can't quite make up their minds how they feel would get pretty annoyed at the Federal government for letting it happen."

They discussed the possibilities at some length and by the time they had made their last observations of the darkening brush country, they knew what each was supposed to do. Maybe it would work. Maybe it wouldn't. Nothing could be worse than the way things stood now.

"I'm going it alone if we can't work this out," Baird reminded them. "That's my job. I'll give it a try."

They were almost back to the dying fire when Luis

said, "There is a thing to remember, Captain. The men who carry out the orders of Hickey. They may be many, in separate groups. I think they have divided in search of Sergeant Flood. We know of the group that found him. Word will have gone out to the others that he is coming to this place. Do not forget that new bands of outlaws may come along at any time."

"You're such a cheerful friend, Luis! Thanks for the happy idea. I can't afford to worry about enemies who are not here yet; there are too many to worry about who are right out there ahead of us."

There was a somewhat different air of tense waiting in the little camp when they rejoined the others. Mrs. Rexford was sitting a little apart from the others, frowning slightly as she watched the close conversation between the other two women. Dirk was standing ominously close to the prisoner.

Baird waited to see if anyone would start explaining what had gone wrong. No one did. Mrs. Davenport broke the tight silence with an attempt at that coyly personal smile she had tried on him before. "Something in the pot," she said. "We opened airtights." Her gesture toward the empty cans near the fire suggested that some sort of hash had been concocted of whatever canned food had been found available. Only the coffee smelled good.

Supper was consumed in silence, Baird's attempt to learn something from Pat Rexford turning out badly. All she did was to shake her head and murmur, "I don't know what they're up to. They're staying away from me."

Finally he decided that it was time to make his move. "We've had a bit of a powwow, ladies," he announced calmly. "My first plan won't work. We know that. So we've considered the matter of duty. Whether we succeed or we fail, we'll try to do our duty." He wondered whether he sounded as pompous as he felt. It wouldn't do to make this speech sound too good. "We considered the fact that Corporal Warner's duty, thrust upon him, by the way, is not my duty. My sole responsibility, you realize, is for the safety of Mrs. Rexford. If I haven't made that clear—take my word for it. I cannot take her into a fight such as the one which looms ahead. Undoubtedly those desperadoes in the timber will try the same kind of wholesale murder that they attempted before."

To his surprise, Mrs. Davenport interrupted. "I think we have all been discussing that point, Captain. And I don't believe we need to anticipate another attempt like the first one. I've been talking to Private Laniard. He tells me that they had been given orders to kill a woman spy. The man who brought that order was himself killed in a skirmish a few days ago. He was the only one who could identify the person to be killed. So it was decided that the entire company should be wiped out."

"That's how it was," Laniard insisted desperately. "Some of us didn't like it at all but Sergeant Oakes said it was the only way we'd be sure o' gittin' the right one."

"Splendid southern gentleman, Sergeant Oakes," Baird commented. "Always the honorable way to wage war!"

"Please, Captain," Mrs. Davenport persisted. "We do not have time for recriminations—or insults. We propose that you take Mrs. Rexford and slip away from this camp at once. It is your business how to get her through to some safe place. I offer you my promise that we will remain here with the wagons, making no move at all until after daybreak tomorrow morning. Then I shall release Private Laniard and send him up the road to his friends. When they learn that there is no reason for making an attack on these wagons, I am sure that they will go about their business."

This wasn't quite the way Baird had planned it but Warner made a quick adjustment in his role. "They'll hit us, all right," he complained. "Mebbe they ain't keen on botherin' a couple o' Reb wimmen but they'll take a crack at us fellers. They're plumb ornery."

"Don't be any more stupid than the Lord made you!" Mrs. Haislip broke in. "We want to get rid of you when Mrs. Rexford goes. Certainly you don't think we would care to be burdened with such an incompetent as yourself!"

"Ma'am, ye hurt my feelin's."

"I fully intended to! I am certain that there will be loyal Confederates among those guerrilla forces ahead of us. I much prefer to depend upon such men."

Warner grinned at Baird. "She's permoted 'em. They ain't outlaws no more, they're guerrillas. And deserters. Well, I s'pose a gal has got a right to choose what kind o' comp'ny she keeps."

Baird broke in hastily. He didn't want Ethan to spoil matters when what they wanted was actually being handed to them. "We'll do it your way, ma'am," he said hastily. "I think it's an intelligent suggestion. Now let me throw in a warning. We'll leave just as soon as we can get things ready and begin to drift out of camp —one or two at a time. That leaves the camp without night guards. I don't think there will be any attack because the—er—guerrillas will be expecting us to keep a strong guard—but don't take chances. Somebody stays awake at all times, ready to head off trouble."

Mrs. Haislip chose to be indignant at the suggestion. "You do not need to instruct me in elementary strategy, Captain. Please set about the business of leaving us!"

He turned away without replying. Speaking directly to Pat Rexford, he ordered, "Get into something that will wear well for riding through brush country. Carry anything that can be strapped to your saddle but leave everything else in the wagon. We'll have to travel fast and in the dark."

"Can we get past them in the night?" she asked, staring hard at him as though searching for some hint of his real meaning.

"We go around. Luis tells me that there will be no trouble in avoiding the brush country if we swing hard into the northwest. There is no easy trail to the Arkansas in that direction, but by taking our chances with some pretty rocky terrain, we should be able to reach the river some miles to the west of the regular crossing. Take dry rations and make sure you have your canteen full of the best available water. We'll give the horses a good drink before we leave. No more water until we hit the Arkansas."

Warner and the other Colorado men were already making their preparations. One of Mrs. Rexford's extra horses was selected for her to ride—and Dirk managed to strip the saddle from Laniard's horse without anyone noticing. He even managed to rig a makeshift scabbard that would hold Laniard's carbine. Pat Rexford was going to ride as part of the Colorado scouts. She was also going to be armed like one.

With Baird giving the orders, they slipped out of camp, leading their horses and making certain not to pass directly north or east of the still glowing fire. Those who slipped away on the right side of the trail would be all right. Those who went on the left side would have to cross the main trail at some distance from the fire but that part was not much of a risk. Any watcher would see only a shadow and would assume that patrols were out to protect the wagon camp.

They made their rendezvous without incident or delay, about a hundred yards south of the wagon trace and just neatly out of earshot of the camp. It was better to risk the suspicions of those behind them than to betray themselves to the outlaws ahead.

"I reckon we done all right," Warner said hoarsely when they were all on hand. "Now if'n anybody back there wants to git nasty and set the outlaws on us, they'll be sendin' 'em in the wrong direction."

"Not for long," Baird reminded him. "Our tracks

will show. All I hoped to gain was a bit of time—just in case our Rebel ladies happen to feel real angry at us and turn the prisoner loose tonight. In daylight they'll see tracks enough to know what we're up to. By that time we ought to have a good start."

Mrs. Rexford said quietly, "I take it that you are planning to do something about these munitions."

"That's the general idea, ma'am."

"Stop calling me that! All of you! While we're working on this operation together I don't want any nonsense. I'm Pat to everyone. Is that clear?"

"It'll save time," Baird agreed dryly. "And we don't have any too much of it. So let's ride. Luis. Lead off. Ethan rides behind him. Then Pat. Dirk and I will be the rear guard."

Mrs. Rexford offered a protest. "I seem to be the only one who hasn't had the plans explained. I think I'll ride with Captain Baird for a short distance while he tells me just what we are hoping to acoomplish."

"Suits me fine," Baird told her. "Dirk, you'd better handle the rear."

They moved off into the gloom of the night, leading their horses until Luis passed the word to mount. It was during this slow period that Baird got his explanation made. "It all amounts to this—that I wanted the women back there at the wagons to believe that our only interest was in getting you safely to the Arkansas. By tomorrow morning, when the bushwhackers start looking for our tracks, they'll soon know what we're trying to do."

"Which is?"

"Get rid of those guns before they are used to kill a lot of settlers."

"Sounds pretty suicidal," she murmured.

"The other way wouldn't be any better. Luis tells me that there is no passage to the river in a northerly direction. If we were trying what we let them think we were trying, we would probably be overtaken. Since they outnumber us pretty badly now, we'd have no chance of getting clear."

"Suicide either way."

"Maybe not. We had two chances. Stick with the wagons and bust right into an ambush. Cut for the river and get lost—then overtaken. This is a third chance. We go for the arms cache. If we're lucky and manage to destroy the arms, we've still got a lot of enemies between us and safety. I figure that our only chance is to have them coming in to attack us while we're holed up with plenty of guns and ammunition. I think we'll stand siege—if we're lucky enough to get into position before somebody else does."

Her faint murmur sounded almost like a shudder. "It seems like a rather desperate plan."

"It is. I'm sorry to be taking you into this kind of danger but I couldn't come up with anything that sounded better to me."

"I'm not complaining about that point. I understood long ago that I might find myself in plenty of trouble before I could reach the nearest fort. I'll not make it any more difficult for you than it already is."

"Good girl."

They rode on through the blackness of the moonless night, only the creak of leather and the crunch of iron on gravel breaking the silence which had become tense with foreboding. For Baird there was an odd mixture of emotion in the night. He knew the dread of a man going into real danger, but he could also work up a warm feeling toward the men who continued to aid him. The Colorado men had no real responsibility. Probably no one would ever know if they elected to leave the area and go back to the assignment which had been given them originally. Their willingness to assume a share of the danger was the difference between a hopeless situation and one where some kind of desperate effort might accomplish something.

He knew that Luis had led them out of the arroyo country and was heading across flat prairie. They were moving in a more easterly direction now but he could still see no sign of the timber land which he understood flanked Perdito Canyon on the west.

After a while Pat Rexford called softly, "Wouldn't it be better if we knew exactly what you plan to do, Captain? We're all expecting to help, you know."

"Sorry. I don't know. I'm simply counting on Luis getting us to Perdito Canyon before Flood brings his outlaws. I think he may have trouble persuading his gang to split up while they've still got an ambush planned. With any luck we can be at the cache before Flood makes a move. How we get to the guns and grab them is something I can't hope to plan until we find out how many of those Cimarron Thunder idiots have been left on guard."

"Suppose the first move is successful? Is it your idea that we can destroy the munitions and escape before Flood and the others cut us off?"

"No. That part I'm planning pretty definitely. I simply don't feel that we have a choice. If we're in retreat we must expect to fight a running battle against odds. I think we'll have a far better chance to stand and fight at the cache. Like I said before, we'll stand siege while we've got plenty of materials for the purpose."

"Real bright idee," Warner remarked cheerfully from his shadow ahead of them. "We sit tight on some kegs of powder and dare them rascals to shoot at us." He didn't sound a bit unhappy at the prospect.

"You know the old military adage," Baird retorted. "The smart general makes the other side do their fighting on the ground he has picked for the fight. I'd rather have them attacking us where we've got an advantage than at some spot on the open prairie or even along the Arkansas. That's not the big consideration, however. I want those munitions destroyed before they can become the means of setting this whole frontier ablaze. The only way we have a chance of doing it is to take a few risks. All we can do is hope to keep the risk as small as possible."

"That's all I wanted to know," Pat said calmly.

Chapter 13

Until a little after midnight the travel was fairly easy.
They stopped twice to rest the horses and to stretch
weary muscles. At the first halt, Luis explained what
he was trying to do. They had moved off at an angle
to avoid detection by the bushwhackers, then had swung
eastward. Now they were headed straight toward Perdito Canyon, angling away from the Cimarron Trail
and keeping about the same distance from the Arkansas.

Just before the second halt, they began to ride through
brush timber and mesquite. Again Luis explained. This
was the edge of the brush country which was the approach to their goal. Perdito Canyon ran roughly
north, feeding into the Arkansas some ten miles from
their present location. Somewhere in that ten-mile
stretch would be the arms cache.

The ride became much more difficult as mesquite
grabbed at legs and even faces. Some of the trees were
just high enough so that the horses plodded beneath
spreading limbs and riders had to fight off the clutch-
ing branches. Twice Baird heard Pat Rexford gasp in
dismay at some sort of mishap but she made no com-
plaint. They rested again after two solid hours of this
sort of difficulty and Luis said that they were getting
very close to the upper part of the gorge. There were

two possible places for the arms to be hidden, he thought, always assuming that the men who had moved the stuff would want it well concealed and under guard. There must be safety from accidental discovery. There had to be water for man and beast, graze for the horses.

"We try to move straight to the upper gulch," he told them. "Unless I have allowed myself to be deceived in the darkness we should be very close to the spot which I think should be the hiding place. We will try to be there as close to dawn as possible. I think it is going to work very well."

"You're the boss," Baird reminded him briefly. "Handle it your way. However, when we reach this gulch I think you'd better take Dirk or Ethan ahead with you as an advance guard. The rest of us will drop back. We can follow you along the canyon, I think."

"You don't need to make special arrangements for my safety," Mrs. Rexford protested at once. "I think it will be better all around if the entire party remains in close contact."

"Who asked you?" Baird asked, trying to sound gruff. "Luis is boss now. Don't try to tell him how to run things."

"*You* just did. And don't think you'll change things by trying to sound grumpy. I know how you're thinking."

When he made no reply, she spoke directly to Luis, using Spanish. The New Mexican laughed a little but then announced, "Everyone will please to remain close behind. I wish that no one should become lost."

"I guess I made a mistake," Baird commented as though talking to himself. "It's not very smart to put a man like that in charge, a man who can't keep his head where pretty women are concerned."

"Thank you for the latter part," she said primly.

"What did you tell him in Spanish?"

"Not very much. I simply reminded him that we were practically cousins—by adoption. I didn't think he should leave me in the rear to get lost. Now stop trying to make jokes to keep me from being nervous. And stop trying to keep me out of the more dangerous places. I'm as much a part of this operation as any of you. Maybe a little more. Try to keep it in mind. You have no responsibility for me as a woman, only as a messenger."

"Now who's trying to make who feel easier? But thanks for being smart about it. Let's move on, Luis —er—General."

When the first gray of dawn let them see the dreary outlines of the land about them, Baird rode ahead to talk with Luis. He made no gesture toward the others and no word was spoken but he saw how Warner and Dirk immediately took positions in the rear. They had been working on that routine most of the night, he knew, taking turns at napping in the saddle so that the man in the rear was always the more alert one. At the same time they usually tried to keep Mrs. Rexford squarely in the center of the line.

The little column was in open country again and Baird could see a shallow valley on the right, cottonwoods, willows, wild plum and similar small brush timber thick on its slopes. "How come we're up here on high ground, Luis?" he inquired. "How do we know we're not riding right past the cache? There's plenty of brush down there to hide a lot of things."

"You forget, Señor," Luis replied with some formality. "I said that the only way to bring wagons to this canyon is by way of the Cimarron Trail. It would not be good to bring them the way we rode tonight. They would have to go up the trail farther, then come across to this canyon at one of two points northeast of here. I believe they would have used the shorter of the two routes. Thus they would be along the canyon some distance ahead of us. They would have no reason to come this far upstream."

Baird grinned. "Don't sound so damned patient with me. I know you went over that before. Now I see the

country and I can understand it better. It seemed like
a good idea to make sure I had the right idea. How
far ahead should we reach the spot where the wagons
came across?"

"A very short distance. You understand, this is a
guess. Wagons could come up the canyon from near
the mouth of it. There is no trail since no one comes
here. Wagons would have to find the best way possible to them. I think they would have used the short-
est route because that one would get them away from
the Cutoff Trail as quickly as possible. Out there they
risked detection even with the regular traffic being so
scant. Call it two miles to the point where they would
have reached the canyon."

"Why canyon? This looks like a swale to me."

Luis smiled. "Perdito is a small canyon. At the
Arkansas it is a meadow. Up here it is, as you say, a
swale. Only where the stream cuts through higher country is it deep. That part is close ahead. It is on the
high ground that wagons could be brought across to
the canyon rim."

He rode a few yards in silence, staring into the gray
of the morning as though trying to pick out half-for-
gotten landmarks. "Señor, I have been thinking," he
commented after a few minutes. "Wagons and a cannon could easily be hidden in the gorge itself but I
do not believe they are down there. It would be most
difficult to take them to the bottom, still more difficult
to get them out. If I had been in charge of the business I think I would have done what I now believe
was actually done. I would let a few people believe
that the cache was at the bottom of the gorge—just
in case of trouble—but I would want everything up
on the rim where it could be removed swiftly."

Baird nodded. "I've been considering that very point.
The matter of a swift move, that is. So get on with
your bright ideas. Does it help you decide where they
hid the stuff?"

"I think so. Only a little distance ahead of us is the

end of this high country I mentioned. Anyone who rides along the canyon rim must swing wide to avoid climbing over a rocky hill. This hill is either a high part in the canyon wall or a knob which marks the end of the high ridge, depending upon how you think of it. There are trees among the rocks. Water can be brought up from the canyon itself. It seems like the perfect hiding place."

"And it's this side of where that wagon route would end?"

"It might well be the end of the route. It is the top of the ridge which wagons would travel." He pointed ahead. "Already you can see the higher ground. Not the first long slope; that is just the way the ground rises and forms the canyon below. At the top of the rise there are rocks and trees. That is the place. Beyond it the ground slopes down again and is flat all the way to the Arkansas."

"You mentioned two possible spots for the cache. Where is the other?"

"Downstream another mile. I have already decided that it is not the second one. I think perhaps there was false information given so that the second one would seem like the true one—but is not."

"But who would get this false information? Why should they give out any information at all?"

"This is only my guess. I think there are many people being brought into this scheme. The Cimarron Thunder part of it was supposed to attract many recruits. The planners did not know who would be trusted. I think they told part of the truth. Not all of it. Not accurately. Perhaps Oakes and Billings received such wrong information."

"And Hickey. It seems reasonable that the original plotters would have tried to protect themselves with some such stunt. It might give us a little more time—if we get lucky."

They continued to discuss the possibilities as they began to hit the gradual up-slope. Baird could now see the stream at the bottom of the gully. There were little riffles showing white water and he knew that the gulch became deeper as its sides grew higher. This would be the beginning of the real canyon.

Then the cover began to thin out and Luis signaled for a halt. The rocky, timbered ridge he had described loomed as a barrier across their path and Baird could see how it tapered away into the northwest from a high knob which was part of the canyon rim. "If I guess right," the New Mexican told them, "there will be men at the cache, whether it is this place or the other. I do not expect that they will be keeping a very sharp watch on this side but there is still the risk. The rest of you should remain here out of sight while I take a look. If all is clear I will motion for you to come on."

"Don't run into a bushwhack bullet," Baird warned soberly. "That ridge would make fine cover for an ambusher."

"I always take very good care of me," Luis retorted with a grin. "Watch and you will see how cautious I am."

They watched but they saw very little. Almost as soon as he swung away from the rim, he disappeared. The rest of the party dismounted and took time to ease cramped muscles. The night had been tiring and they were a red-eyed crew. Pat Rexford was stalking about gingerly in a pair of faded infantry trousers, one leg of which had come loose from the boot into which it had been tucked. Both the trousers and the gray shirt were a little too large for her but she did not seem to be concerned over her appearance. Strands of dark hair had been torn loose from her braids by the brush they had come through and there was a long scratch across one dusty cheek.

She caught Baird's appraising glance and murmured, "I suppose I must look as horrible as I feel."

"Don't fish for compliments. You're just right for this job."

"Thank you—I think. Do you know what annoys me most at the moment? That water down below—and us up here full of sand and grit."

"Keep thinking that way. The dust is like the fleas on a dog. Keeps you from worrying about other things. By the way, I've got an order to give—if you'll accept one from me while our commander is out scouting. In case we have to make any kind of attack here, your job will be to take care of the horses."

When she started to protest, he cut her off sternly. "Every cavalry unit has men assigned to hold the horses. It's the regular routine. Men who draw the job obey orders. You'd better try to do the same."

"Yes, sir," she replied meekly. Then she added, "I know how much of a problem I have become, Captain. If I sound like a woman, don't let it worry you. I'll try to keep out of the way."

He gave her a full smile then. "Seems like I ought to expect you to sound like a woman. Even in that ragbag outfit you still look like one."

He moved away quickly, edging forward to a place where he could see across the bare country along the rim. There had been no sign of Luis since he disappeared into the mesquite but presently Baird saw movement on the knob and moments later Luis appeared in full view, motioning for them to come forward.

"Here we go," he called back to the others. "Luis seems to have decided that this side of the ridge is safe. We'll stay close to the rim but not too close. If anyone is down there along that creek I don't want them to look up and see us."

"Do you suppose the cache is somewhere close?" Pat asked as they rode forward in a little knot. "I've been mighty curious about all of the private conversations between you and Luis."

"Sorry," he said, speaking to all of them. "I should have kept you posted—as I said I would do." He explained it all as they walked the horses toward the steeper slope ahead. "Now it seems as though we may have guessed wrong about this being the place. Either that or the cache is on the far side with no guards on this side."

"I think that is the way of it," Mrs. Rexford said quietly. "The men with the wagons came in from the Cimarron. They expect to move out in the direction of the Arkansas. If there is good cover on the other side of this ridge, there would be no reason for them to take the extra pains to come across to this side."

"Sounds like the lady thinks things out real good," Warner chuckled. "I'm gittin' real glad that she's on our side."

Baird did not reply. He could agree but he didn't say so.

Dirk put in a word. "I figger it's right here—on the far side. Luis kinda moves like he's excited."

"You can all stop guessing," Baird told them. "Luis will soon tell us what we need to know."

He rode out ahead with Warner as they began to work their way through the tangle of rocks and bushes which marked the beginnings of the steeper slope. Luis had not reappeared so both men kept guns ready. Baird even turned to motion for Dirk and Pat to wait. Luis had signaled clearly enough but there was still the chance that he might have been trapped after making the signal.

They slowed a little, both of them beginning to show their uneasiness, but then the New Mexican appeared, jumping from one ledge to another as he came down toward them. Baird saw where the horse had been left in a patch of high bushes so they swung toward it, meeting Luis there. It was Warner who called out cautiously, "Anybody on the other side?"

"It is as we thought. Some of the cache cannot be seen from the top of the knob but I saw enough. There are two wagons down there, also a pile of something under canvas. Perhaps it is the cannon and also boxes of ammunition. I could not be sure."

"What about guards?"

"I could see none. That is natural. Men would not be showing themselves if they were alert. Also they would probably be asleep somewhere if they are not alert. We cannot assume too much."

"Anybody in sight down below—in the canyon?" Warner persisted.

"I could see little of the canyon from up there. But the canyon is of little concern now. We must surprise any guards who are there by the wagons. I think we can do it. There will not be many of them, I think."

"We play it as safe as we can," Baird reminded him. "This is no game."

"You have a plan for attack?" Luis inquired.

"Nothing very definite. We'll have to talk it over and then see how things shape up. You're the one who knows most of what it's like over there. You'll have to pass on suggestions. My best guess is that two of us ought to cross the ridge and work down to where you saw the wagons. I feel certain that these are the wagons we want but we'll have to make sure before we make a real move. Also we'll have to know how many guards were left with them. While we're getting that part sized up, the others can ride around where the ridge is lower. They'll have to make a big circle so as to stay out of rifle range. When they get out into the open on the far side of the knob, I want the guards to see them but not at a distance that will have them doing any shooting. While the guards have their attention held there is a chance to take them by surprise."

Warner chuckled. "Ye learn real good, Cap'n. It's the same scheme us fellers used on ye the other day."

Baird grinned. "I didn't say I invented it. You boys can claim all the credit."

He repeated his plan for the others and Mrs. Rexford promptly offered an objection. "What happens if you find that there are more guards on duty than two of you can handle, even by surprise?"

Baird shrugged. "We have to take risks. There's no safe way of handling this kind of a job. If anybody has a better idea, now is the time to suggest it."

"I have one," the lady said promptly. "You told me a while ago that I was to be the horse holder. I think I should do it. Why shouldn't I appear in the open alone—with the horses, that is? Two of you can be coming down from the top of the ridge. The other two can move in along the far slope after crossing at a lower point."

"I don't like the sound of it. What happens if they gallop out to grab you before we're in a position to stop them? They might not try it if there were three of you. If you're alone, they might."

"I've already thought of that. It will be a matter of timing. I suppose you and Luis are intending to make the direct approach?"

"I think it would be right."

"Then the rest of us will ride to the left and cross the high ground at a safe distance. When we see open country on the far side of the ridge, I will take over the horses and wait while the two men with me move into position. By then, you and Luis will have had more than enough time. When I ride out into the open, that will be the signal for you to close in."

"It is good strategy," Luis said soberly. "The wagons are hidden close under the knob, near the canyon rim. I do not think any part of the cache is far from the canyon. Such a flanking movement should not run into trouble."

"You're the boss," Baird reminded him. "If that's the plan, I'm in favor of it."

"He's the boss," Warner agreed dryly. "But he'd better keep an eye on this gal; she'll be stealin' his jób if'n he don't show up mighty smart."

Chapter 14

Baird laughed along with the others but he couldn't feel that there was much to laugh about. He didn't like many parts of the plan. There was too much he still didn't know about the arms cache and its sentinels. If there were only a few guards, the strategy would be all right. If the guards had been reinforced, there would probably be a hard fight—and Pat Rexford would be alone where none of them could help her.

She seemed to be reading his mind. "Don't fret about it, Captain. Nobody likes the choice but we have to do the best we can. That's why we came here, isn't it?"

"I suppose so. Just remember that I'm not doing what I really ought to do when I let you risk this move. I could . . ."

"I'll try to keep your conscience clear," she assured him with a thin smile. "I'll be very discreet."

"You'd better be! Put slip knots on every lead rope. If you get chased, let the horses go. Get away!"

She shook her head. "That order I do not accept. Those horses are your only chance of escape—if this turns out to be a hornet's nest. If I am pursued under circumstances which make things look really bad, I'll

131

circle back toward the part of the ridge which we propose to cross. Come to that point and rally there."

He simply shook his head. There was no point in arguing with her. Nor did he have much choice. He was depending on her cooperation so he had to depend on her judgment as well. Somehow he felt that she would do the smart thing no matter what happened.

"Take my carbine," he told her after he had turned his horse over to her. "On this kind of a job I prefer to depend on the handgun. Have you ever operated a Sharps?"

She took the weapon, studied it for a moment and then worked the action carefully, seeing to it that it was not loaded. "I've seen these," she said quietly. "I've never fired one, but I know how. What about ammunition?"

He dug into a pocket and handed over a half-dozen paper cartridges. "You won't need more than these, I hope. You know about the primer?"

She nodded and he turned away before he could show too much worry. Luis was already starting back up across the ledges and Baird hurried after him. Over his shoulder he called guardedly, "We'll try to get into position well before you do. Then all you'll have to figure on will be your own relative movements. We'll wait until Mrs. Rexford shows in the open. Ethan, you and Dirk try to be ready at that same moment. Take your time and don't risk any wrong moves. If we don't handle this part right, we're done."

It seemed to Baird that the ridge was just one boulder piled on top of another. Somehow a variety of bushes and trees had managed to get their roots into the crevices so that the pile of rock had become a wooded hill. When they reached the top he could see a good stretch of the barren country along the crooked length of Perdito Canyon. They were not far from the Arkansas, he knew, but the land showed little of the grasses which grew along the river. The willows and cottonwoods which he had seen farther

up the Perdito were no longer visible. Probably such
vegetation grew down in the canyon near the water,
but up here on the rim there was the same gray-brown
desolation which marked much of the Cutoff Trail. A
few tufts of grass, some dwarf cactus, here and there
a forlorn bit of runty juniper. The exception was this
little knob. Apparently some freakish underground
spring came to the surface where the rock layers below had buckled into a narrow ridge. The seepage
supported a timber growth found nowhere else in the
area, not even on the extension of the ridge itself.

"Go very quietly now," Luis warned in a hoarse whis-
per as they began to see the tops of fair-sized trees
below them. "Very quickly now we see the wagons.
They are over to the right, beneath the tallest of the
trees. I think they cannot be seen at all by anyone
along the lower rim of the canyon. Only from up here
above them."

Baird was impressed at sight of the big pines growing on that northeast slope. Whatever underground
water welled to the surface up here among the rocks
had to be ample for such growth. Oddly, it was heavier
on this side than on the other even though the ridge
itself was not many yards across. It had made an excellent place for the die-hards of the Pecos Volunteers
to hide the wagons. With very little difficulty they
could move from this base into any part of the Arkansas valley. The main part of the Santa Fe Trail
was vulnerable to attack. So were a couple of under-
manned military posts and perhaps a dozen small settlements. To the people of Colorado and western
Kansas, this stock of munitions was like having a
bomb in the cellar.

He murmured softly as he spotted the wagons, Luis
pointing a finger to direct his gaze. Then both men
began to work into a position which would let them
approach the spot under the best possible cover. At
first Baird could see only what Luis had reported, two
freight wagons and what appeared to be a canvas-

covered small cannon. By the time they had crawled over the first bare ledge and were working into a real descent through heavy brush, he knew that there was at least one more spread of canvas below him. The outline hinted at long boxes there, probably rifles or muskets. Either the original handlers of the munitions had unloaded a third wagon here or some of the stuff had been brought to the spot on mules. There was quite an arsenal here along the Perdito.

"Not a soul stirring as far as I can see," he whispered in Luis' ear. "No sign of a tent or shack. If they have guards on duty, where do they house them?"

Luis did not reply, knowing that Baird was simply thinking aloud. They eased cautiously down the slope, the effort to stay in the thickest cover causing them to lose sight of the wagons completely. A rock ledge with a sheer drop forced a more extensive detour and when they were again moving beneath trees and through thinner brush, they knew that they were almost on a level with the wagons. They could even see a bare slope opening out toward the downstream rim of the canyon. That was when they heard a rasping voice growl a disgusted, "Damn!"

Both of them froze, relaxing again swiftly as the unseen speaker went on, "How the hell do ye keep gittin' so lucky, Buck? I dunno why I play cards with ye! All I do is lose."

A throaty chuckle sounded in reply and a deeper voice rumbled, "Yo' ain't got no call to complain. Yo' ain't losin' nothin'. Yo' got nothin' to lose. Anyway, there ain't another Goddam thing to do up here. A man can't sleep all the time."

"Hell! We shoulda gone with the others. They didn't need to leave guards here. Nobody comes through this damned mizzuble country. We mighta had some fun if'n we'd been with the others."

"Mighta got ourselves shot up, too. Stop bellyachin'! Ye'll never git a easier chore."

"I'd ruther be movin'. And 'fore long we oughta be.

When the boss gits enough men rounded up we'll be on our way. With all o' this stuff here to rig out a fightin' force we'd oughta plumb raise hell with the Yanks."

Under cover of the rumble of talk, Baird and Luis moved closer. They could see the wagons again and within seconds they could see the vague figures of the two men on guard. No other guards appeared to be on duty and the fragment of conversation seemed to confirm that fact. From this lower level Baird could see several smaller piles of equipment under canvas. This was even more of a cache than he had believed it to be. If Biddleton—or any other ambitious guerrilla leader —had managed to recruit as little as two hundred men, he could have set the whole frontier ablaze with so much equipment. Quantrill's raids in Missouri would have looked puny by comparison.

"Still looks like only two guards," Baird whispered, "but we'll wait until our decoy stirs them up. Then they'll holler for help, if they've got help around."

"Don't wait too long. Not when the trouble starts," Luis hissed in reply. "I know one of these men. The one who talks caution is Buck Hubbard and he is not cautious at all. He shoots very quick. I do not know how many he has murdered. Two lawmen have died trying to arrest him."

"I'll keep it in mind. Now let's get a few yards apart. We'll edge in a little more but not much. When you know they've spotted Mrs. Rexford, jump in without waiting for any talk. I'd like to take a prisoner, but we don't risk anything on this job."

"No more than we risk already," Luis corrected.

They edged forward again, putting a little distance between them. From his new position, Baird could see the two men who lounged on the ground with a tattered blanket and some dirty cards between them. His question about a tent or other quarters for the guards was answered then and there. Canvas had been fastened to one of the wagons to provide shelter beneath the vehicle. So far as he could determine, there were no horses or other stock in the area. Probably the original draft animals had been taken away by the other members of the band, perhaps concealed somewhere down in the canyon where the graze would be sufficient for them. In that event, there would be other guards down there. It was a point which needed remembering.

Suddenly the taller of the two men scrambled to his feet. There was a blurred exchange of words as both of them spoke at the same moment. Then Baird was moving. He heard one of the guards say something about trouble, then the other snapping, "Damned if'n it don't look like a woman in pants. What the hell's goin' on around here?"

He could see that both were staring out through the screen of trees toward the open country along the lower canyon rim. It was easy enough for Baird to get into close range while they were so intent on what they were seeing in the opposite direction. When he was directly behind them, only some ten feet distant, he barked, "Hold it right there! Get your hands up high!"

One of the men obeyed the order almost automatically. The other stopped in his tracks but brought his hands up slowly and only to shoulder height, slowly turning his head as he made the move. Baird recalled the warning Luis had given him, so he was ready when the half-raised right hand made its swift move downward. The outlaw jumped to the side as he clawed for the gun, but the attempt to get out of the line of fire didn't work. Baird fired, knowing that the heavier blast of Luis' pistol had sounded at the same instant. He saw the man go down but turned his attention swiftly to the other guard. "Don't try it!" he shouted.

Luis ran forward then, his dragoon pistol still smoking. He rolled the dead man over with his bare foot, hastily squatting down to pick up a six-gun almost like Baird's. "Buck was very swift," he said calmly. "The gun was out already." Then he sidled over to snake another six-gun from the holster of the second man.

"Call the others in," Baird ordered. "But be careful. Make sure that we haven't overlooked any more polecats."

Luis kicked aside the canvas flap which had transformed the freight wagon into a tent. "Two lots of blankets," he announced. "Nothing under the other wagon. I think there were only two."

"Ye're right," the captive grumbled. "Jest the two of us. If'n that damned Buck hadn't been so all-fired cocky, we'd ha' had more. But not fer Buck! 'Cordin' to him all he needed was comp'ny. He could hold the place all by hisself! Him and his fast gun!"

Luis moved back to him then, his tone almost sympathetic as he murmured something about pride being fatal. There was nothing gentle about the way he made a search of the grumbling prisoner.

"Nothing," he reported when he was satisfied. "The usual things. He fooled me. Sounding so unhappy I thought perhaps he might have a hideout gun."

"Just so we know," Baird nodded. "Now shout for the others to come in. They've been yelling questions ever since we fired those shots."

Luis pushed through into the open to hail the approaching Mrs. Rexford, Warner and Dirk, while Baird motioned for the prisoner to walk away from the wagons. "Just so you stay out of any trouble," he told the bearded scoundrel casually. "No use shooting you if I don't need to."

The man shrugged, lean shoulders hunching up under his long, shaggy hair. He was dirty, gaunt, unshaven and generally disreputable, but there was an odd quirk of humor in his glance. The pale-blue eyes seemed interested in what was happening to him but not particularly bothered. "Don't seem like I'd figger to start nothin'," he told Baird. Buck didn't make out so good—and Buck was the one what called hisself the gunman."

"And also the better card player," Baird added.

"So ye heard me bellyachin'. Must be ye was listenin' a spell."

"A spell."

"What's yer stake in this, mister? And what the hell are ye doin' with a female in yer gang?"

Baird shook his head. "You're forgetting something, friend. You are not the one who asks the questions around here. You answer them. Be thinking about it—and think hard. One of our boys thinks he's a mighty tough questioner."

He could see something like fear come into those pale eyes; the prisoner had mainfestly lost some of his whimsical humor. Baird waited, gun poised, until the others came in, most of their questions already answered by Luis. Then he said, "Dirk, how about taking charge of our prisoner? Take him over behind the trees where Mrs. Rexford won't have to watch. Then find out what he knows. Use your own judgment. While you're persuading him a little, we'll see what we've got here."

The prisoner had apparently been thinking pretty hard. It seemed to puzzle him that no harsh threats had been made. This matter-of-fact assumption that he would have to be beaten was worse than an open threat. "Look, folks," he protested. "I ain't fixin' to bleed none fer this business I'm in. I don't give a damn one way or another what happens. Ye don't need to git rough. I ain't aimin' to hold nothin' back."

Baird nodded casually. "Then tell the lady. Dirk, stay with him and see that he uses nice polite words. If you think he's lying—" He nodded toward the clump of trees he had indicated earlier.

Then he turned his back and motioned for the other two men to join him in making inventory of the plunder. "We don't try to haul any of it away," he reminded them. "Let's look it over and see if we can figure out the best way of getting rid of it. One good fire would do the trick but we can't chase ourselves right out into

the open that way. Too many people would like that
quite a lot."

Warner climbed into a wagon while Luis uncovered
the largest pile of boxes and crates. Baird made a quick
inspection of the cannon. When they had exchanged
reports they went back to where Dirk had tied the
prisoner to a tree. The man could sit down with some
comfort but both hands were pulled tight by the rope
which went around behind the tree trunk.

"Let's hear it," Baird said crisply. "Tell it again. The
lady will listen to see if you tell it twice the same way.
If we catch you in a lie . . ."

The prisoner nodded helplessly. "I ain't lyin', mister.
Like I said, this ain't no skin offa my nose." He talked
rapidly, nervously, the story coming out with a ring of
truth. He had been a Texas volunteer at the time of the
Sibley expedition. His company had been assigned to
the Pecos detachment which was to join Sibley in the
attack on Fort Union. There had been two hundred
men, seven wagons with baggage, ammunition and extra muskets with which Sibley planned to arm the New
Mexicans he hoped to enlist. There was also a mountain howitzer.

Sibley had failed to reach Fort Union and he had
failed to find recruits. A messenger had ordered the
support column back down the Pecos. They had left the
ammunition wagons and most of the muskets and the
cannon behind, partly because they were retreating in
something of a hurry after the alarming news from
Apache Canyon. Rather than be slowed by wagons,
they had cached the heavier stuff on a little creek. He
didn't know the name of it.

Later some of Sibley's officers had come up with a
plan to use the arms cache for another attempt at in-
vading the Arkansas valley. A few men from the original force were to be the nucleus of this second
invasion. The prisoner had been one of them. They had
come up the Pecos with horses and had moved the
supplies to this present location. Two of them had been

left as sentinels while the rest went out to recruit and to guide expected units to the hideout. He agreed that the originator of the scheme was a Captain Biddleton but he insisted that he had not heard of Biddleton's arrest by Confederate authorities. He also agreed that the project was to be known as Cimarron Thunder, the army as the Pecos Volunteers.

"Who's in charge now?" Baird demanded. "It's not Biddleton."

"I dunno. There was a feller name of Hickey at Fort Union. The Feds wasn't on to him and . . ."

Baird exchanged glances with Pat Rexford. "Sounds like Hickey is playing a sort of double-double-cross. He's using the remnants of the Cimarron Thunder force to set things up so that his plunder gang can steal the arms."

She shook her head. "It seems incredible that he could pretend to aid the Cimarron Thunder plan and then send men out to attack those who are in it."

"Maybe he's having trouble keeping both parts of his gang satisfied. Somebody must be smart enough to see what he's doing." Suddenly he swung to face the prisoner. "When you fellows moved that stuff up here, was it Hickey who gave the orders?"

"No. I never heard about him then. Biddleton ordered it."

"When did you first hear about Hickey?"

"Not long ago. And then I wasn't sure where he stood. We figgered at fust that them recruits what was drillin' in Mace's Hole would rally around and help out with this scheme. Nobody rode back in here to tell us how many of 'em they'd rounded up. Jest one feller showed. He said as how a man named Hickey was gonna see to it that we made planty o' loot outa this deal. That's all I know."

Baird nodded as Mrs. Rexford shot him a questioning glance. "I think that's probably the size of it. Hickey took over when Biddleton went east under guard. With the Cimarron Thunder crowd he pretended to be carrying on Biddleton's scheme. With his pet cronies he schemed to steal these arms for a plunder expedition. It would be easy enough to murder any of Biddleton's men who didn't want to join him."

The prisoner started to ask a question but Baird ignored him. "Luis," he said sharply. "If you were going to be under attack along the Perdito and had a choice of battleground, where would you set up defenses?"

"Down the canyon about a mile," the New Mexican told him promptly. "There is a better place than this knob. It would take many men to defend this spot."

"Even with a cannon?"

Luis shrugged. "Who knows about cannon?"

"I do. At the Academy they supplied us with a lot of exercise like firing howitzers. This gun is old enough so that its operation is familiar to me. Do you think we can defend this knob with it?"

"The other place is better. We can be flanked here. Down the gorge there is—" He had turned to point as he made his explanation. Suddenly he broke off and the others knew why as they followed his gaze. A number of tiny figures showed at the base of a dust cloud. The next part of the performance was about to start.

"Flood?" Warner asked.

"I'd expect it to be," Baird told him. "Even if our Reb friends didn't jump the gun, he'd still be making his move in a hurry. I guess it's too late to find a better place."

Chapter 15

Baird's orders came out without hesitation. There had been a lot of odd changes in the command of this little army but he knew that the others would expect him to take charge now. "Get that cannon wheeled out! Dirk, you and Luis see if you can handle it while Ethan and I rustle up some ammunition. If you need help, holler." He swung to stare at the prisoner. "Where are the shells and the powder bags? Which pile? And don't waste any time. That gang coming up the rim will be just as anxious to bust you wide open as us."

"Sorry. I don't know nothin' about it. Better look in the boxes near the gun."

Baird was already aiming for that batch of stores. "The powder ought to be in flannel bags, Ethan. Likely red flannel. We want some of them and some iron balls big enough to fit the bore of the howitzer. You'll recognize 'em when you find 'em. There'll be a wooden block attached to each ball. That's the wad."

He was prying open a box as he spoke. When he found only layers of musket cartridges, he turned to another pile, assuming that the rest of the first stack would be all cartridges. None of the boxes carried markings so the only thing to do was to keep looking.

"Iron balls over here," Warner called out. "With wooden wheels fast on 'em."

"Good. Shove 'em over toward the open space where the boys are moving the cannon. Now where in hell are those powder bags?"

Over his shoulder he called to Mrs. Rexford. "Lend a hand, Pat. Climb into that wagon and pry open a few boxes. We didn't look too closely at first."

When the hasty search produced no howitzer powder, he changed plans swiftly. "Too late to play with the cannon now," he told them. "That party down the canyon is going to be closing in just as soon as they look us over at closer quarters. We've got to buy ourselves a little time by using a different sort of trick." He pointed to the wagon Mrs. Rexford had been searching. "Let's get that wagon out to the top of the slope. We'll try to turn it into a self-propelled bomb."

"Mostly kegs of powder in here," Pat reported. "Also some boxes of cartridges and a case of muskets."

"That's fine. Let's get the wagon into place first. Then we'll bust up some powder kegs. Everybody on a wheel. I want to line it up so it will roll straight down toward the rim. By using the gap they seem to have leveled out for bringing the wagons up, I think we can do it about right. Plenty of slope to keep it moving once we get it started."

He explained the rest of the idea as they worked, getting added suggestions from the others. Dirk's idea was probably the most practical. He simply brought a couple of the saddle horses and used ropes to turn them into a team. The wagon came around into position much more easily after that.

"Stupid of me not to think of it," Baird told him. "Glad somebody used his head." They had to work the wagon into position by sheer effort even after it had been swung out to the top of the natural ramp, but finally it was ready to roll, stones under the wheels holding it for proper loading and timing. Warner and Dirk began to secure the front wheels against any ten-

dency to swivel, using ropes and muskets in an elabo-
rate but practical web of tie rods. Then the wagon
tongue was raised as far as possible and lashed into
position like some vengeful pointer. The vehicle had
become simply a four-wheeled load of trouble. It
couldn't be steered, only aimed.

Meanwhile Baird and Luis had been breaking open
a couple of the powder kegs and using the loose powder to spread around among the loose musket cartridges
they had been throwing into the wagon. "Lay it on
thick," was the only order Baird issued. "The bigger
the fire the better. I don't know how long it will burn
before everything blows up but let's have everything
burning—just in case she runs over the cliff and doesn't
explode. I want this stuff ruined beyond any possible
use."

They threw in a few cases of muskets on top of the
other broken boxes and Baird started to calculate his
timing. There was no way for him to judge how long it
would take for the loose powder to burn its way into
becoming a real explosion but he didn't think the time
would be great. They had to have the wagon some distance from the knob—and really rolling—before any
fire could be set to it. Otherwise the whole scheme
might become fatal to everyone now working for its
success.

By the time he was ready, the riders out along the
rim had begun to spread out a little. Obviously they
had seen the wagon being worked into position and
couldn't understand what was happening. Twice they
had halted as though to discuss the problem, but now
they were fanning out as though to form a skirmish line
for the actual attack on the ridge.

"I make 'em a quarter of a mile," Warner announced
as he saw the way Baird was staring. "And it's Flood
on our right, sure enough. We git her aimed at the
middle and no matter which way she veers she'd oughta
hit somebuddy. Ain't nothin' to do but hope now."

"I gotta 'nother idea," Dirk announced. His grin

suggested that having been praised for his thinking, he was anxious to come back for more. "Let's load that dead varmint on the wagon seat before we start it rollin'. We'll tie him up so it'll look like he's aimin' the thing. That oughta make them riders git a mite curious."

Nobody even offered to argue the proposal. Baird was glad enough to be rid of the corpse and he could see some merit in the idea. The other two men seemed to think it some huge joke. They promptly hauled the dead man to the wagon and lashed the corpse into position on the seat, a rope about the neck holding it erect. Mrs. Rexford looked a little sick as she watched this callous handling of the dead man but the prisoner seemed to have no qualms whatever. From his sitting position at the base of the pine he jeered, "Good ole Buck, the one-man army. Now it looks like he's almost gonna make it. Gonna be as dangerous as he always liked to figger he was!"

"All ready," Warner called, jumping to the ground. "And we'd better turn it loose. Them polecats is gittin' damned near into musket range."

"Everybody clear," Baird called. "Kick the chocks away. Luis, trade guns with me. No, not the one you took from Buck. I want that dragoon pistol of yours. Make sure it's loaded."

They made the exchange as the wagon began to roll slowly across the first stony bit of slope. Warner used a musket barrel as a lever to correct the angle of the front wheels when they saw that it was aimed a little too far toward the canyon, but then speed began to pick up and further effort became useless. "Back to the trees!" Baird shouted. "Be ready to cover me with some gunfire if I need it." He was climbing to the tailgate of the accelerating juggernaut as he yelled, trying to get a good grip with his left hand while he used the right to drag the big pistol out of his belt.

When he was in a position to see through past Buck's swaying body, he knew that the aim was still good.

There was a slight tendency for the wagon to curve toward the canyon but its general course was still toward the now puzzled riders ahead. They had halted their advance and were shouting warnings at each other. Baird had a feeling that what bothered them most was that hunched figure on the seat. The dead man had become the apparent driver of a pretty weird device.

Back on the knob there was a stir of activity, somebody running across an open space and somebody else bringing a horse into view. Baird had no chance to take a good look in either direction. The wagon was picking up speed on the downgrade. He had to make his move now or risk injury in jumping off.

He made sure that he was clear for his jump, then aimed the big pistol at a shifting pile of loose gunpowder. The shot brought an instant flare but he was clear, rolling on the rocks and getting scraped up pretty well before he could get control of himself.

For a moment he was tempted to stay there on the ground. If the burning powder should set off an explosion sooner than he had hoped, it might be as well to be right where he was. Just as quickly as the thought came to him, he decided against it. Distance was more important. He scrambled to his feet and started running hard toward the wooded ridge. That was when he saw Pat Rexford riding toward him down the slope the wagon had used.

He tried to wave her back but she came on, ignoring both his gestures and the rattle of gunfire which came from the milling group of outlaws. Baird glanced over his shoulder long enough to see that they were still not quite sure what they ought to do. Some of them seemed to be firing at the wagon, evidently taking aim at the man who seemed to be driving it straight at them. The rest were simply shooting. Three or four even drove their ponies in as though to intercept the smoking contraption, but others had turned as though to retreat

from it. The sight of flames licking away the canvas top
was hint enough for the smart ones.

He saw Pat swing a little to her left as though she
intended to ride back toward the knob. That was what
he had been waving for her to do, but he still felt a
small tinge of disappointment that she was letting herself be frightened away by harmless shooting. Then he
knew that he had not given her full credit. The change
of direction had been for quite a different purpose. She
swung again, this time as though to go around him,
and he knew what she had in mind. She was going to
bring the extra horse right past him, headed in the
proper direction. Instead of coming up, halting, then
starting the retreat, he would have a horse moving in
so that he could swing into the saddle and head for the
knob without so much as a stop. Sometimes it was
amazing how many ideas this woman had picked up
while living the sort of peaceful life she had described
to him.

"Nice work, General," he told her as he grabbed the
horse and swung himself into the saddle. "You sure do
figure things out."

"My job," she called back to him as she sent her
horse in a dead run for shelter. "Remount service. Remember?"

Baird dug in the spurs and was putting distance between himself and the rolling wagon when the blast
came. He could feel the horse break stride but that was
all, the concussion only helping to keep up speed. He
saw Pat grab for a saddle horn but she didn't look
around. They simply kept low, feeling the heat beginning to beat at them as they headed for the rocks. A
few bits of debris dropped close but neither was hit
and soon they were clear of the danger area.

Behind them he could hear the continuing explosion
of musket cartridges and then another blast somewhat
less violent than the first one. He guessed that a keg of
powder had blown up after a few moments of delay,
probably burned through after failing to rupture in the

first explosion. Another one roared as they reached the trees and swung in beside the other men.

Baird looked back only after he had slid from the saddle and helped Pat to the ground. She was shaking slightly but it seemed to be more from excitement and triumph than from fear.

"Nice work," he told her. "You hauled me out of there just about in time."

Before she could reply, Ethan ran up behind her and began to slap at the seat of those baggy infantry pants she was wearing. "Sorry to git familiar with a fightin' gal," he chuckled, "but yer pants was on fire. I reckon some o' that blazin' junk caught up with ye."

That broke the strain a little and they all turned to stare at the smoky mess along the canyon rim. It was impossible to tell exactly what had happened and the others could offer little information. The wagon had blown up just when it seemed that the whole load would go over the rim into the canyon. "Mebbe it was part way over," Warner said. "And mebbe the two of ye kin count yerselves lucky that it was that way. If'n she'd blasted wide open any closer—and up on the level—ye'd likely have more to show fer it than a burnt hole in a pair o' pants."

"What happened to Flood and his gang?" Baird asked.

"They took out hell fer leather—jest about the time the lady got the hoss to ye. We seen 'em high-tailin' it down the canyon rim and then all hell busted loose. We ain't been able to see nothin' through the smoke since then but I reckon some of 'em got singed real good. They was mighty close when she blew up."

"Let's make some moves," Baird said sharply. "Some of them will have come through all right. Now they'll be out for blood. We've still got to expect some fighting."

"Got any more bright ideas like that last one?"

"I'm working on it. We'll rig up the second wagon just about the way we did the first one—only don't spill any powder around until we are ready for whatever it is we decide to do. I don't want to get cooped up here in any kind of fight and have a loaded wagon standing beside me all ready to blow up."

"Still want to figure on the cannon?"

"If we can find those powder bags. There won't be time to make up charges—and I don't remember how much of a load it's supposed to take."

As an afterthought he called, "Don't bother locking the front wheels. We won't get another chance to use this wagon like we did the first one. Just make sure that there's stuff in there that we want to destroy."

"We should expect them to try a flanking move," Luis said soberly. "I think we should have a sentry on the top of the knob."

"I'll go," Mrs. Rexford offered. "I can raise an alarm as well as anybody else."

Baird shook his head. "Can't spare you. You're getting to be such an expert in the remount department that . . . All right. I won't make stupid jokes. Luis is the one who ought to be up there. He's right about the chance of attack from that point. We can't afford to let somebody else do what we did. Luis, see if you can locate a rifle among these stores. Or a rifled musket. You know the ridge. Maybe you can set up where you can discourage anybody who tries to sneak up from the rear."

"One gun ain't gonna be much good," the prisoner told them gruffly. Baird had glanced briefly at him after the explosion and knew that the fellow was impressed but badly frightened.

"You know something you didn't tell us?" he demanded as he stared hard at the man.

"I reckon so. A Mex what useta deal with the Comanches went out to see if he couldn't persuade some o' the heathens to join up. We got word a couple o' days ago that he was movin' in with about forty of 'em. The feller what brung the news went on west to locate some of the other recruitin' parties. Seems as how we didn't want to have too damned many renegade red-skins around here before we had a purty good crowd of our own."

"Nobody trusts nobody," Baird commented. "Which is probably the only way to handle it. When do these renegades figure to get here?"

"Mebbe today."

"Thanks for the warning. Now you won't have to take Buck's job on the second wagon."

He ignored the man then, turning back to find Pat Rexford eyeing him impatiently. Before she could say anything, he said, "I didn't try to spare you when I sent Luis on the sentry job. I'm trying to think ahead. This howitzer can keep us alive if we find the right use for it. The men will be needed for small-arms fire. I want you to get some training as a gunner. I'll explain while we hunt for those powder bags."

They began to rummage through the piles of boxes, finding more musket cartridges which could be loaded onto the second wagon along with a dozen cases of Enfield muskets. There were already several kegs of powder in the vehicle so they could figure on using it somewhat in the way they had used the first one.

"This is what is known as a twelve-pound mountain howitzer," he explained as they worked. "The powder bag fits into the back of the bore—which is smaller than the actual bore which fits the twelve-pound shell. A full gun crew goes through a pretty complicated drill for such a small piece of artillery so I'm trying to explain it all in such a way that we can double up on some of the moves. The powder bag goes in first. Then it's rammed hard into the back end of the barrel. After that, the iron ball goes in—with the wooden plug between it and the powder. There's a Bohrman fuse attached to each ball, as you may have noticed. When the gun is fired the flame of the explosion leaks around the ball and ignites the primer. The primer must be cut to a proper timing before the ball is inserted. Then the ball—which isn't a ball but really an iron case full of powder and sulphur and musket balls—explodes at the proper time after leaving the gun. I'll explain about firing the gun when we find some powder bags."

"Start explainin'," Warner shouted. "Here's them damn bags."

Chapter 16

Warner had found a stack of boxes containing the howitzer charges. There were gunnery tools also, including ramrods, swabs for cleaning the bore after firing, priming wires, and friction primers.

"We're in business!" Baird exclaimed with satisfaction. "Ethan. You and Dirk better get in on this little gunnery lecture. I don't know how we may be able to use this little brass monster, but if we need it there won't be time for more instruction."

"I ain't so sure I want to git eddicated with one o' them things," the Vermonter grumbled. "Every war pitcher I ever seen showed dead gunners hung across cannons."

"Pay attention. Maybe you'll be luckier." He motioned toward the cannon. "First thing we need to do is set it level. Lend a hand and we'll shift it around until she's got her feet on the ground just right."

They helped him to swing it until it was pointing toward the burning wagon. Then they scraped here and there until the level was achieved. "Now," he went on, "we figure on elevation. A howitzer doesn't have much muzzle velocity. The idea is to lob the shell in an arc, letting it drop on the target. We set the fuse for the time it will take the shell to get where it's going. Both time and elevation have to be right to get the job done."

"If it requires so much precision, how do you expect to do it correctly?" Pat asked.

"Trial and error. I remember a few numbers so I'll start with a sort of guess. We'll adjust from there. For a starter I'll try a three-degree elevation. Bring the stuff over closer and we'll practice a bit."

"Try extry long shots fer practice," Dirk suggested. "I jest seen riders beyond the smoke. Mebbe ye'll hit one of 'em."

Baird grinned. "I'll try four degrees. Now, let's get on with gun drill. Pat, shove a bag of powder into the muzzle. Ethan, take a ramrod and push it down as far as it will go. I'll put the shrapnel shell in—and set the fuse. Somehow I seem to remember three seconds as the time that would go with four degrees of elevation. We'll try it on for size."

They loaded as he prompted them. Then he explained how the priming wire was used to puncture the powder sack so that a spark could reach the powder. Finally he adjusted the friction primer, rechecked aim and elevation, motioned the others clear of the gun— and pulled the lanyard.

The boom of the little gun seemed deafening but all of them recovered from the moment of shock to move aside so that they could see past the cloud of muzzle smoke. Baird was in time to witness the explosion of the shell somewhere beyond the heavier smoke caused by the burning wagon wreck. "Careless," he grumbled. "I should have remembered that I wouldn't know much about results if I couldn't see where the shell hit. I'm not even sure whether it hit the ground before it exploded. Warner, how far do you make it to the exploded wagon?"

"Wouldn't be more'n a quarter mile, I reckon."

"I made it four hundred fifty yards. That first shell hit a hundred yards or so beyond. Let's try another one for distance, shorter this time. We're aiming at the wagon. Two seconds fuse, two and a half degrees of elevation. Pat, you're gunnery clerk. Remember the numbers."

"I'll remember something else for you, Captain. Only a few moments ago we were informed that a collection of cutthroat savages were expected to appear at this rendezvous today. We also had a strong hint that certain savages of a different color were hopeful of arriving first. Have you forgotten about that?"

"Shove in a powder bag. Ethan, get ready to ram it home. We'll do our worrying when we see them. Right now we've got to learn how to shoot this gun. It'll take care of a lot of Indians if we handle it right."

She gave a nervous little laugh. "Very well. So I talked too soon. I should have known what you had in mind."

"I'm surprised that you didn't. Mostly you do. Now shove that powder bag in and step back."

They went through their version of the drill four times, the fourth shot exploding squarely in the embers of the burning wagon fragments. There had been no further sight of the retreating outlaws, either because the added smoke blocked the view or because they had disappeared behind the nearest brush cover. Baird checked the elevation and fuse figures with Pat and nodded his satisfaction. "Now we get ready for what might happen next. If we have to defend this ridge, we'll make the best possible use of the cannon. If we get a chance to slip away, we'll take the gun with us and use it to blow up the rest of these munitions from a safe distance."

"What about this other wagon?" Dirk asked. "It's all primed to stir up as much ruckus as the other one."

"We wait and figure things out a bit. I want to know what Flood's gang is going to try next. Then I want to see if anybody else is going to show up. It's hard to tell how we'll have to operate."

Luis yelled a warning. His lookout post was not close enough for them to hear more than a part of what he was trying to tell them. Baird quickly ran out into the open but for a moment or two he could see nothing but smoke. Then he glanced to his left and saw what was bothering Luis. Seven more riders were coming toward the knob from the west, apparently riding the ridge trail which Luis had mentioned.

He watched until he saw three others come from behind the smoke and gallop to meet them. "Ten of them now," he called back to the others. "I think we put some of the first batch out of action but they're getting help."

"Hickey's men," Pat said quietly as he rejoined the group at the wagon. "Otherwise they wouldn't be joining each other without some show of fight."

There was a conference out in the open and then the combined outlaw force began to fan out across the ridge. Warner seemed to take on new energy. "Looks like it's fixin' to be our kind o' fight. Dirk, you and me better git into them bushes about thirty yards on the left. We'll send Luis out a little farther." He turned to bawl orders to the lookout and promptly got a reply which indicated that the New Mexican was already on his way down to the probable battle line. "Baird, you'd better stick right here and make sure that they don't try to fool us by swingin' around at the last minute and makin' their real try right here."

"Good thinking, Corporal," Baird told him briefly. "Pat, you'd better get up on that wagon so you can see out across the top of the brush. I'll try to get in at least one round with the howitzer. I'll set the shell to explode at about three hundred yards and aim about that same distance to the left of the burned wagon. I'll be firing blind so you'll have to tell me when they get into range. There won't be time for anything very fancy. Meanwhile, keep that carbine handy and have extra cartridges out."

She climbed obediently, calling out when she was standing on the wagon seat, "What happens if they break through our defense and get among the trees?"

"Then we'll have a hell of a fight on our hands. I

hope you can fire that carbine as well as you handle it. But forget about that part. Just give me warning when some of those bandits get within about fifty yards of where you think my shell is going to explode."

There was silence while he heaved the gun around, prying it into its new alignment, checking level and elevation, then checking the wheels to hold it in place. He went through the loading routine, reciting the drill half aloud as he tried to make certain that there would be no error.

"They're coming toward us," Pat called to him. "Spreading out as though they plan to cover this whole side of the ridge in their attack. I've got a landmark out there which I think will be about right for our purpose."

"Good. Just hope some of them hit it. Maybe I'll hit *them*."

He waited silently and then she shouted, "Fifty yards short of target. Two of them coming straight at it."

He grinned at the businesslike tone and readied the friction primer. He was counting to himself when Pat shouted, "Fire!"

He yanked the lanyard and raced for the wagon as the gun bucked from its position. The boom of the exploding shell came long before he was in a position to see anything, but Pat reported excitedly. "The burst was right among them! I think at least two men went down."

A riderless horse galloped toward the canyon rim as he watched. Three of the attackers swung toward the smoke cloud as though to give aid to someone Baird could not see. Warner's yell of delight came from the brush. "Good shot! Ye busted 'em up a mite."

Baird leaped to the ground and began to re-aim the cannon. He had scarcely gotten it back into its original position when Pat called out, "No time for that now. They're going to cross the ridge. I think they've given up trying to attack from this side."

Warner's shout confirmed the guess. "We got to git back to the other side, Baird. They're circlin' to git behind us."

"I'm on my way," he yelled in reply. Then he stared hard at Pat. "Sorry to leave you here alone but that's the way it's got to be. I hope you're as good a carbine marksman as you are an artillery spotter."

"Don't expect too much," she told him with an attempt at a smile. "I'm really just remount troops, you know."

"And keep an eye on the prisoner. He's tied up loose."

"What am I supposed to do about him?"

"Use your own judgment. Crack him over the head with one of those muskets if he even wiggles suspiciously. Or shoot him. We wouldn't miss him." He hoped he made it sound ruthless enough for the man to be impressed.

He moved deliberately into the open, running along the edge of the brush so as to move in an arc inside of the one the attackers were now riding. On the stony plain he could see seven men still on their horses. Behind them, where smoke and dust indicated the spot where the shell had exploded, he could see two inert forms in the dust. Still another man was hobbling away to the north, trying desperately to catch a horse that was also limping. The little brass howitzer had done a lot to reduce the odds, even with those extra outlaws on hand.

Warner ran out to meet him, both men showing themselves in the open as they moved to meet the next attack. "Might as well let 'em know that we're goin' to keep in front of 'em no matter where they come in," the older man panted. "Luis and Dirk are doin' the same thing only not out in the open."

There was a pause and then he grinned briefly at Baird. "It musta took some o' the ginger out of 'em to have that shell bustin' 'em up."

"They're still getting ready to attack," Baird reminded him. "We can't let 'em get onto this ridge."

"Flood's drivin' 'em. I reckon it was Oakes what started this circlin' business after Flood got kinda discouraged when the wagon went up. Ye got Oakes with that cannon shot, by the way."

"That's fine—but I don't like the way they've rallied for a new attack. They're in a big hurry. I've got a notion Oakes and his men brought word that they had to do their job fast. Maybe they've found out about some more Pecos Volunteers coming in."

"Likely. But right now it's this gang we got to stop."

Baird pulled up then, watching the way the line of outlaws continued to form that wide flanker movement.

"They're not going to come up the ridge," he declared. "They're going to go all the way around. I'm going to cut straight across. Tell Dirk and Luis."

He was climbing as he shouted the final words. He could hear the exchange of yells between Warner and the other two, but the sounds died away and he knew that they were continuing with the effort to work along on an inner line parallel to the circle the outlaws were making. It did not take long to reach the summit at this point and presently he could hear the voices again. Then he saw the seven riders. They had cleared the lower slope of the ridge and were having some sort of conference, apparently settling on their point of attack.

"Git ready!" Warner's voice sounded. "Looks like they'll hit straight in from there."

Baird scrambled down to a rocky ledge, trying to find a spot where he could see through the brush. It happened that the first really clear spot which permitted him to see any amount of open space also allowed him a good look at the far side of the canyon. The sight was not pleasant.

"Indians on the far side of the gorge!" he yelled. "They're riding downstream. Almost opposite us. Thirty or forty of 'em."

"Ain't got no time to look now," Warner yelled

back. "We got to do somethin' about the bastards on this side."

Baird moved still lower and suddenly saw that he was directly in the line of attack. All seven of the enemy were driving hard at the point he had to defend. Apparently they had decided to concentrate their attack at a single point, hoping to penetrate the brush and give themselves some of the cover advantage which the defenders enjoyed.

Warner was issuing crisp orders again, bringing in the other two men. They moved with caution, however, and the timing proved to be exactly right. When the attackers split into two separate groups it worked out that three of them were charging straight at Baird, the other four galloping in at the point where Luis and Dirk had concealed themselves. Warner was in a position to fire at either group.

A single shot came from somewhere on Baird's right but he held his fire, knowing that the six-gun was useless at such a range. He had to let the enemy get into the first bit of brush country before he could hope to fight effectively.

They seemed to be thinking along that very line, for they began to blast away as they started up the first slope of the ridge. Baird kept low and waited, hearing slugs whine from the rocks on both sides of him. Only two shots had been fired from the hill itself. It seemed likely that Luis was also waiting to make effective use of the revolver he had taken from Buck.

Finally they were close enough. Too close for comfort. Baird raised himself quickly to firing position and began to shoot, forcing himself to take dead aim in spite of an overpowering urge to trigger the shots as fast as the revolver would work.

He was lucky. The first slug knocked an attacker right out of his saddle. Then a second man yelped in pain, slumping to the horse's neck as he tried to turn the mount for a retreat. The third outlaw almost fell out of his saddle in a frantic move to get away. Baird threw a shot at him just to keep the panic on him, then he reloaded and moved across to where the other attackers had entered the timber. At once he saw two riders beating a hasty retreat from that spot but he could not see what had happened to the other two— or to his friends.

Suddenly Warner's voice called a hoarse warning. "Hold it, Baird. They got him pinned down. Don't git into the line of fire."

As the final word died away, two shots sounded in unison. Luis announced calmly, "That is it. Take the gun of the first one, Dirk. Make a search. I take this one."

"It's Flood, ain't it?" Dirk asked.

"Flood it was. Now it is a dead man."

Warner called out promptly as Baird closed in behind him. "Hustle it up, boys. There's Injuns across the canyon. Let's git back to the wagon."

"Anybody hurt?" Baird asked as the others came toward him.

"Nary a scratch," Dirk assured him cheerfully. "How bad did you git it?"

Baird looked down, feeling a little stupid at sight of the blood on his left hand. There was a dark patch on his sleeve just below the elbow and suddenly he realized that it hurt.

"You shouldn't have told me," he complained wryly. "I didn't know I'd bit one off. Now it hurts like hell."

"Pull yer sleeve tight," Warner advised. "It ain't bad or there'd be more blood on yer hand. We'll look after it when we're back on the other side."

"We can't leave this side unguarded. They might try again."

"Them?" Warner jeered. "Look at 'em makin' tracks. I reckon they seen them Injuns and that was all they needed to make up their minds. With Flood and Oakes not around to prod 'em, they ain't got no guts fer more fightin'."

"The one who retreated from in front of me was the

prisoner," Luis remarked. "Laniard. I think Flood's
men came first, perhaps starting during the night. That
is why they arrived so soon after us. Oakes came with
the others after they found our tracks this morning."

Baird nodded, trying to keep his mind on the next
problem while he climbed the rocks. It was not much
better than thinking about the wound in his arm but it
was more practical. "You figure things out real good,
Luis. Now start figuring how we'll beat off forty renegade Indians."

Chapter 17

They climbed silently, taking a breather when they reached the top of the ridge. Then Warner asked, "Do ye figger these redskins is part o' that Cimarron Thunder business?"

"No doubt about it. The prisoner said that Indians were expected today or tomorrow. I'll bet they're a fine band of tribal outlaws! The chiefs are still trying to keep the peace but there will always be a few warriors who won't take orders."

"Kinda like Biddleton hisself," Ethan muttered. "The Reb gov'mint stopped him but it couldn't stop some of his cronies. Now they've hooked up with a gang of Injuns jest like 'em."

"So—we get ready for another fight. Luis, where will they be likely to cross the canyon? Assuming that they're aiming for us, of course."

"They will be," Dirk glowered. "They could hear the shootin'."

Baird was holding tight to his injured arm as they slid down to the level of the munitions cache. The arm was beginning to throb from the exertion but there still wasn't enough bleeding to cause him any great worry.

Luis answered after a moment of thought. "There is but one good place near here. The opposite wall of the canyon has a path perhaps a mile downstream. Horsemen could descend to the stream there, then come up the canyon about the same distance. It would be quite easy to climb from the bottom to the rim right here. They will use the path which I imagine the guards have been using for getting water."

"Good. Maybe we've got a chance."

"I'd like it better if'n we had more'n a chance," Ethan declared. "I kinda hanker after real good odds when I'm bettin' my hide."

Pat Rexford broke through the bushes to meet them then, her anger and breathlessness apparent. Then she saw the blood on Baird's arm and the anger changed to swift concern. "Let me look at that!" she panted. "Sit down! Now!"

Baird glanced comically at Warner. "New boss," he said briefly. "Keep going. I need to get rid of a shaky feeling anyhow. Finish loading that wagon. Anything except howitzer ammunition. And leave a keg or two of powder for the final cleanup."

"Ain't ye figgerin' to let the wagon set off the rest of the stuff?"

"No. I want it out along the canyon rim where Luis says those red hellions will be coming up out of the gulch. Move, man!"

"The prisoner escaped," Pat broke in. "I couldn't stay still down there when the fighting started. I had to come up to see if there was any way I could help. When I looked back he was gone."

Baird pulled himself erect. "We'll let this doctor business wait until we're back at the wagon. With a loose enemy—who had his choice of guns before he left—I don't think it's smart to get separated."

She started to argue but had to hurry to avoid being left behind. Baird gave her the word on the Indians. "This must be the gang of renegades that the Cimarron Thunder plan called for in the first place. The ex-prisoner said they were coming."

"What tribe?"

"Probably from several—although I'll bet they're mostly Comanches and Kiowas. Outlaws of the tribe who won't obey tribal law. Just like the white outlaws we've been fighting."

"How many of them?"

"Thirty—forty. I was too busy to count."

"Too busy getting yourself shot," she fretted. "Sit down on that rifle case and let me cut the sleeve away."

He tried to ignore the twinges of pain as she began an expert cleaning of the shallow wound. It helped him to forget the discomfort to tell Warner and the others how he planned to use the wagon of explosives. Instead of planting it as a sort of fuse in the cache itself and exploding it by cannon fire from a safe distance, they would reverse the procedure. The wagon would be taken out to the rim, the cannon held in its present position.

"Not much choice," Baird said grimly. "We can't figure on going anywhere for a while. Not with a cannon anyway."

The three men were working rapidly to improvise harness and to add various combustibles to the wagon's load. Warner was calling the plan a "firecracker bear trap" and he seemed as excited as the two younger men.

There was one interruption as Dirk pointed to the northeast and shouted, "There he goes. He's got a gun but he's on foot. Should I git after him?"

Baird looked and saw that their former prisoner was running hard for the canyon trail which had suddenly become so important to them. "Let him go," he said indifferently. "Unless he's a mighty good friend of that Indian recruiter he's not likely to reach the bottom of the canyon. Those renegades are likely to shoot him first and find out about him later."

Luis had estimated that it would take about forty minutes for the Indians to find the path down into the canyon, pick their way over the rocks in the stream bed and climb the switchback trail which led to the rim on the near side. Forty minutes to get the wagon down from the knob and to the proper spot. Forty minutes for Baird to get the howitzer ready. This time there would be no ranging shots. He had to do the job exactly right first time.

In ten minutes the wagon was being eased down the rocky grade with a makeshift team, Warner handling the clumsy brake while the other two kept the horses pulling in the proper direction. Twice they had to use muskets as braking bars to keep the vehicle from running away from them, but they managed it without a major accident. By that time Pat had put a bandage on Baird's wound, using strips of cloth taken from some sort of garment she had carried in her slicker roll. He didn't ask what the garment had been. He knew that it probably had been a prized possession of some sort. She had brought so few things with her that anything in the package had to be of some value.

As soon as the arm was attended to, he went to the task he had been forced to neglect. "Thanks," he told her briefly. "Now you'll have to be most of the gun crew. First, let's get the gun aimed at the approximate spot we want to hit. We can do the final touches when they spot the wagon. Also, you can move a few of the shells and charges over to the gun."

"I hope you made the right decision," she said quietly. "I keep thinking that we might have been a little safer if we'd moved the cannon out to the rim so we could cover that trail the Indians will have to climb."

"You're thinking that we'll be in trouble if any of them get to the top?"

"Of course. I'm also wondering what will happen if that vital first shot misses. We'll actually be supplying them with weapons."

Baird grimaced, partly from the pain of using the arm. "Don't make it sound so bad. They've already got more than enough weapons to wipe us out in any kind of stand-up fight. But you're forgetting something. We couldn't use a howitzer to fire down that path.

This kind of gun is good for just one thing, to lob a shell up in the air and drop it on a target."

"Are you sure?"

"Take my word for it. Even if we could fire the gun downward we'd have to have proper equipment and a good gun crew. The crew would be exposed on the rim of the canyon, subject to sniper fire from the slope and the far side. Believe me, this is the only chance we have."

They were silent then, getting the gun settled into position for final aiming. Working with one hand made things difficult but Pat surprised him with a show of strength and also with the deft way she used one of those musket pry bars. The gun was in place and they had established a fairly good level when they heard the gunshots to the east.

Baird's first thought was that the renegade savages had found a quicker method of crossing the canyon, but his first look told him the truth. Warner and the others were retreating from a dozen riders who had appeared from the same direction Flood and the others had used.

"Now it gets complicated," he muttered. "Either the outlaws have found another lot of reinforcements or this is the original Cimarron Thunder crowd. I hope we don't have, to explode the wagon to keep them from hitting us. We'll need it a lot worse for the other purpose."

He saw the way she was staring fearfully out toward the open country where so much seemed about to happen and he went on, "Sorry I tried to do it this way, Pat. My first job was to see that you got clear. I should have done it and left this stuff to somebody else."

She turned quickly, staring straight at him. "Who else would do it? This is far more important than me. The lives of many, many people depend on what you —we, are trying to do."

Before he could make any reply, she looked away

again. "I wish our men would get out of there. Warner isn't even looking at those new outlaws."

Baird took a second look. The retreat from the wagon had ended. Luis and Dirk were circling a little to the left of the wagon as though preparing to defend it. Warner had taken charge of the extra horses but was standing between the wagon and the rim of the canyon, staring down. "He's drawing a lot of slugs toward that wagon!" he muttered. "Why doesn't he get away—or swing out from the wagon the way Dirk and Luis are doing?"

"Give him credit," she told him, a new ring in her voice. "I think he's being smart. I believe he's timing his retreat."

Baird's grin came slowly. "Maybe you're right. And he's right about it. Our best bet is to have both parties converge on the wagon at the same time. Ethan was right when he called it a bear trap. Maybe we'll catch two bears at the same time."

"Optimist!"

"I'll go a bit farther. Putting up a show of fight at the wagon will make that new crowd more interested in the wagon itself. I'll offer odds that Warner and his boys don't even get chased very hard when they make their retreat. The wagon is going to seem too important."

He forced his attention back to the howitzer, lining it on the wagon and making sure of its level. "Five hundred yards, give or take a very little bit. It's not far beyond the ruins of the other one. Three degrees elevation. Two and a quarter seconds on the fuse. That ought to be right on the bulls-eye."

He set the shell in the muzzle, Pat having already rammed home the powder bag. Then he stood ready, priming wire in his hand. For safety's sake he preferred to hold the two final steps until Warner and the others were clear.

"The outlaws have been bluffed into stopping," Pat

said half angrily. "Now maybe the strategy won't work."

Baird studied the scene in front of him, seeing that Luis and Dirk had put on too much of a show for the newcomers. Now there was a new problem. Instead of fighting off an attack, the two Coloradans had to find a way to get the outlaws to come on.

Warner gave his signal then, yelling to the led horses and presenting a picture of complete panic as he broke for the cover of the ridge. The other two promptly followed his example, their retreat sheer flight.

At least that was the way it must have looked to the hesitant outlaws. They took what seemed to be their cue and galloped straight at the wagon. Baird rammed home the priming wire and set the friction primer. To break the tension he felt mounting within himself he ordered gruffly, "Get another shell handy. Powder bags under cover!"

Dirk drove in first. "Get ready," he yelled. "Ethan's got it figgered. The Injuns oughta pop over the rim jest about the time when them other polecats reach the wagon."

Baird grinned. "Ethan's a fox. I hope I shoot as well as he figures."

There was what seemed like a long delay. The outlaws slowed their pace as though beginning to have suspicions of a trap. Clearly they did not suspect the true nature of the trap for they continued toward the wagon. They were still a hundred feet short of it when the first swarthy figure came up out of the canyon. The fellow didn't look like an Indian but Dirk offered a quick explanation. "Ethan says there's a bunch 'o cutthroat outlaws and 'breeds with 'em."

Warner and Luis were in the clear by that time but still Baird waited. A gun fight had broken out at the wagon now, Indians pouring up from the canyon and blasting away at the men who seemed to be riding to drive them back. In a matter of seconds a real skirmish was in progress and Baird took time to enjoy the fact that the two groups so busily engaged in killing each other were probably recruits for the same plot. Cimarron Thunder was being split on its own treachery.

"Shoot!" Warner yelled. "We got 'em now."

For a moment more Baird hesitated. Both sides out there were suffering casualties. It seemed well to let them continue as long as possible. If the first cannon shot should miss, it might spoil the whole thing.

Then the outlaws began to give way. That was when he pulled the lanyard.

With the roar of the gun, everybody seemed to move at once. Warner jumped away from the smoke, trying to see the result of the shot, but each of the others rather surprisingly remembered the brief lesson in gun drill. Dirk rushed in to swab out the bore and get rid of lingering sparks. Pat lifted a powder bag from a covered case and brought it forward. Luis began to lever the cannon back into the spot where it had been positioned before the recoil dislodged it. Baird never had a chance to compliment them. The explosion of the shell set off a whole series of blasts which told him what he wanted to know. He had scored a hit.

They were ready for a second round by the time the muzzle smoke had drifted away. There was no definite target now, only a fiery mass of smoke and flying wreckage. Still, they got off the second round. If there were survivors out there who still might have any ideas of attacking, it seemed like a good way to make them think again.

"That's enough," Baird told them when he saw that they were getting ready to repeat the performance. "Let's have a look. Then we pack up and get ready to move. No use crowding our luck. We don't know how many more of these guerrilla bands will be arriving." Then he sat down and let his arm ache.

For a little while he wasn't sure just what was happening. He felt tired all over and the smoke around him seemed to have turned almost black. When an arm went around his shoulders he was not sure whose arm it was. He didn't even care.

"Get your head up!" Pat ordered briskly. "I can't pour water uphill. Swallow a little of this."

He drank from the canteen she held at his powder-blackened lips and felt a little better. "I'll be all right—but don't stop holding me up. It's a real nice idea."

She took her arm away promptly, rising to speak with Warner. "Corporal, I think you should take charge of whatever must be done next. Captain Baird is not himself."

Warner's chuckle sounded clear above the continuing noise of distant explosions. "Mebbe ye don't know what he's like when he's hisself, ma'am. Somehow he sounded real sensible to me."

"Nonsense! We still have many things to do. There must be a number of wounded men out there. Even though they are outlaws they must have attention."

"We'll fetch 'em in, ma'am," Ethan told her hastily. "Come on, fellers."

The last crackles of exploding musket ammunition died away as the three men rode down toward the rim. There was an almost eerie silence for perhaps a full minute, then two shots rang out so suddenly that it brought a little gasp from the woman.

"No worry," Baird told her. "Survivors still shooting each other. Maybe it's just as well. We've got no way to handle wounded prisoners."

"We shall certainly have to make an attempt. I have have had no compunction about helping with the killing of those horrible creatures, but if they are now wounded and helpless I feel differently about it."

When he made no attempt to argue, she suggested, "I'll help you back toward a more comfortable resting place if you don't make silly remarks. You cannot possibly be comfortable on these rocks."

"It's not bad," he said as she helped him to his feet. "The rocks are hard—but the company's real nice."

She didn't reply for several seconds. Then she asked, "Don't you think you have picked a rather strange time to play at being gallant?"

"Lady," he said soberly. "I'm not playing."

Chapter 18

A few minutes of complete rest chased the dizzy feeling. It occurred to him that he had been on the go almost continuously for four days, getting sleep only in brief snatches. Probably weariness as well as the slight shock of the wound had warned him to ease off a little. The warning, of course, could not be heeded. There were still enemy groups in the area. He had to assume that others might show up.

The three scouts came back promptly and Warner reported that there were no survivors along the rim. "I figger there wasn't more'n a couple what was hurt too bad to git away—if'n they wasn't blowed to bits. A young Comanche musta seen a chance to git some scalps and he went too fur. Wounded feller shot him."

"You saw this?" Mrs. Rexford asked with the shock clear in her voice.

"No, ma'am. We seen the Injun with the scalps. He was dead. So was the feller under him."

"What about other survivors?" Baird asked.

"Mebbe a couple o' the Injuns got down over the rim. We didn't see no sign o' nobody movin'. I dunno."

"Then let's get on with it. Get your horses ready for some more riding. Check weapons. Make sure you have ammunition, water and food. Then we haul the cannon out to the rim. When the next lot of bandits show up here for a look at the cache, I want 'em to see nothing but ruins."

He saw to it that they carried with them three charges for the howitzer, leaving everything else in the pile that had remained after the second wagon was loaded. Dirk amused himself by smashing the locks of some of the remaining muskets against various cases and barrels. It all helped to spread combustibles around and to dispose of weapons which might get into enemy hands.

Finally they rode down the ramp, hauling the little brass cannon along behind them. "We'll fire from five hundred yards," Baird announced. "That's a range we already know something about. We'll set up just a little distance from the wreck of the second wagon. Mrs. Rexford, I think you had better swing out in a little circle and keep watch while we're finishing this chore." He grinned thinly as he added, "Now that you've served your apprenticeship with the remount and artillery branches you might as well take on something new."

"Thoughtful of you, Captain," she told him in a dry voice. "I realize that you're arranging things so that I do not have to get a close look at that scene of death. Thank you. I accept."

"Quite a gal," Warner commented as she rode away from the rim. "I kinda figger the gov'ment knew what it was doin' when they sent somebody to see that she didn't git lost. Likely she'll show some o' them generals back east how to win the war."

"No argument," Baird told him briefly. "Now let's see where we ought to place the howitzer. Close enough to figure on the distance being the same. Far enough away to stay out of the smoke."

They set up the gun quickly enough and Baird checked his figures, allowing for the fact that they were now shooting uphill instead of down. The first shell struck a little low and seemed to bounce right across the remaining munitions. Its blast set fires in the brush. A second shot was directly on target but they fired the final round into the exploding mass of smoke.

"Looks like we stirred up them rocks real good," Warner grunted. "That oughta do it."

Baird nodded. "Luis. Where's the steepest part of the wall on this side of the canyon? I want to drop our little friend over the side. It seems like a shame but we're disposing of everything and I want this cannon busted up like the rest of the stuff."

"Not far," Luis told him, pointing downstream. "That trail from below starts at the base of a cliff. It would be a fine place for the purpose."

They disposed of the gun quickly enough and Baird motioned for Pat Rexford to join them as they headed for the Arkansas. "With a bit of luck we may even overtake those Reb friends of ours before they reach Fort Larned," he remarked. "I'm sure Ethan will enjoy Mrs. Haislip's company again."

"I ain't even sure I'm goin' on to Larned," the Vermonter retorted. "Seems like us fellers have been out of our own backyard long enough. This here's Kansas, ye know."

"Better stick with me," Baird said mildly. "We've got an important government agent to convoy. You'll want to give her time to send some sort of report back to Denver. That'll square you with the boys at headquarters real good."

Warner laughed aloud. "I reckon that's the only reason ye're fixin' to stick with her!"

"Not quite. I'm wounded, you know. She's the nurse."

The afternoon shadows were beginning to lengthen when they hit the downgrade which marked the end of the canyon. From that point to the junction with the Arkansas, Luis explained, the Perdito was just a wandering little creek, its meadows much like the grasslands along the Arkansas itself. There had been no signs of new enemies anywhere along the line of march o they went into camp without delay, all of them too weary to push the worn-out horses any farther.

Scrubbing away powder grime and trail dust helped ome. When they had eaten hard rations and had lenty of the good water available, they began to get hemselves settled for the night, taking advantage of he cover for security against any fresh surprises. The orses grazing in the good grass kept the hideout from eing completely secure but a couple of quick patrols t dusk would take care of the sentry problem. There vas simply no indication of an enemy within miles.

None of them even mentioned the hectic affairs of he day as they went about the business of shaking off atigue and tension. Finally it was Baird who called cross to where Luis was dozing in the late rays of the un. "How far do you think our wagons will be ahead of us when we hit the main trail?"

The New Mexican didn't even move. "Not very far," ne replied. "I think they started late—after the blonde ady sent the second lot of outlaws to catch us."

"Don't say that," Pat warned in mock alarm. "Didn't you notice how much Captain Baird was interested in Mrs. Davenport?"

"That'll be enough from the gun crew!" Baird ordered, glad to see that Pat Rexford wasn't too exhausted to be paying attention. "I agree with Luis that somebody—probably Mrs. Davenport—had a lot to do with the second lot of outlaws getting across to the cache so soon. I also think Mrs. Haislip has contact with Confederate agents. It seems to me that we'd be smart to keep either of them from knowing what really happened today."

"Any good reason?" Pat asked.

"Some. For one thing it's always good policy to keep the enemy fooled, even if you don't fool him on anything important. Give him enough chances to make mistakes and the odds are that he'll make one. Also there's this Hickey character. I'd rather he didn't find out what we did. If he gets the word and goes into hiding, we don't get him. If he thinks his scheme ran into bad luck, maybe he'll hang around until we can arrange for his arrest."

"Sounds good to me," Warner growled. "What kin we do about it?"

"Try this yarn. We tell everybody that Luis talked us out of trying the rough country north of the Cimarron Trail. We decided to swing around on the other side to pass the ambushers. We got lost during the night and in the morning we had to hide out when we saw Flood and some men coming toward us. The place we hid was on the fringe of the ridge. We saw Flood's men attacking some kind of a wagon camp among the trees. There was a real hard fight. Then some more men with Oakes leading them came along. They showed up just as a band of Indians—and some fellows in Confederate uniforms—popped up out of the canyon. Then the big fight started. They were banging away at each other for a long time, Flood and Oakes caught between the defenders of the camp and this Indian force. Then the whole place blew up and we lit out. We don't know what happened behind us but the explosions continued for a long time. Nobody chased us. How's that?"

There were general mumurs of agreement but Pat said drowsily, "You lie very well, Captain. You must have had much practice."

"Thank you, ma'am," he told her politely as Dirk laughed aloud. "It's nice to be appreciated."

"You don't know how much. I've been trying to figure out a way to plan on Hickey's arrest—and I haven't done so well. Now I think I shall sleep better."

They were on the move before the first streaks of dawn, delaying only long enough for Pat to look after Baird's wound. His arm was stiff but he didn't let it bother him too much. The injury itself was minor and he liked the way the nurse was attending to it. He didn't tell her so but he didn't think it was necessary.

She seemed to understand a lot of things like that without being told.

They rode cautiously, Luis out in front and Dirk flanking at some distance from the line of cottonwoods which now marked the course of the Perdito. In midmorning they reached the Cimarron Trail and found the tracks of two wagons already on it. Since the only hoofprints to be seen were those of the regular stock, they knew that there was no escort of any kind. The women were going through on their own.

They overtook the wagons only a little distance short of the Cimarron Crossing—the place where the Cimarron Trail crossed the Arkansas. Baird told his story simply, enjoying the way Mrs. Davenport seemed to be battling with her own thoughts. He was sure that she wanted to pursue a line of questioning but did not dare. To cover her confusion she became elaborately casual and by the time the wagons were on the Santa Fe Trail, the group seemed to be almost back to the earlier routine. Warner was in nominal command. Luis was riding ahead as scout. Mrs. Haislip was complaining about practically everything. The big difference was that Mrs. Davenport continued to ride in Mrs. Rexford's wagon, fishing desperately for information she suspected must exist—and getting absolutely nowhere.

There were no alarms, no trace of riders anywhere along the Arkansas, and the journey became quite amusing to the five people who were enjoying the obvious annoyance of the women who wanted to know and did not dare to ask direct questions.

That was still the situation when Luis came back to report three riders waiting on the trail ahead. Warner quickly issued orders for a more cautious advance but the trio turned out to be a scout party from Fort Larned. When Baird identified himself there was a swift alteration in the suspicious stares of the men.

"Captain Baird!" a burly sergeant exclaimed. "I got orders to be lookin' fer you. The Cap'n's got some kind of message for you."

Then he hurried on, "Maybe you kin fill us in o
some o' the tales we been hearin'. Some folks claim th
Rebs are fixin' to try another invasion of this part o
the country. We got it purty straight. They been tryi
to recruit and they picked some o' the wrong prospect
We got it from men what turned 'em down."

"You can relax, Sergeant," Baird told him with
thin smile. "The threat existed—in a way—but it's ove
now." He repeated the story they had concocted fo
the two women. It would have to be the story fo
everyone until arrangements could be made for the a
rest of Hickey at Fort Union.

It was only when they were actually closing in o
the military post that Baird found a chance for a pri
vate word with Pat Rexford. "The sergeant tells m
that there are papers waiting for me here. I think tha
delayed commission may be catching up with me bu
that part isn't important. I may have a new lot c
orders. If any such orders keep me from going on t
St. Louis with you, I want you to know that one o
these days I'll be looking you up again. Soon, I hope.

She met his glance without any attempt at coyness
"I think I would like that. However, if you chang
your mind I will understand. The past few days haven'
exactly been normal enough for any of us to trust ou
emotions."

He grinned cheerfully. "Maybe it's better this way
emotions being what they are. Nobody had any tim
for spouting a lot of foolish sentiments which mean
nothing."

"I don't remember any sentiment at all," she saic
with an answering smile.

"You don't?" He made it sound almost tragic. "Al
those fine compliments I paid you—about being a good
remount officer, a good gunner, a good scout, a good
nurse . . ."

"Oh, those things. I didn't consider them as compliments. I simply assumed that you were recognizing
clear fact. Now if you had told me I was pretty when I

had a face full of powder grime—that would have been a compliment."

"No, that would have been flattery. I'll try to do better the first chance I get." They were rolling now in between a cluster of ugly buildings. This was the collection of indefensible shacks—empty shacks for the most part—which was known as Fort Larned.

The sergeant, who had preceeded the wagons in to the post, now came back to salute Baird formally. "I'm to take you in to Cap'n McCollum right away, sir. He's plumb relieved to hear what happened out there. You kin see fer yourself that we couldn't ha' defended this post."

Captain McCollum was an elderly-looking officer whose leanness and lack of color helped to explain his rank and position. As an invalid he had been sent to command Fort Larned because he wasn't physically able to handle more active duty. Baird remembered him as a worried, somewhat querulous officer who had seemed annoyed at even being asked for help. Now he was cordial, almost apologetic.

"Sorry I couldn't send men to help, Baird," he told him. "But I hear you got along fine without them. The sergeant tells me that there is no longer any threat to the Arkansas."

Baird decided to try something he had not even thought of when he had stopped here on the way upriver. "I think it's ended. There were to be two invasions. Fortunately for our side, we had two defenses against them."

For a moment he didn't think the thin man would pick up the cue, even though he had given the phrasing a rather odd emphasis. Then he saw that the deep-set eyes had widened a little. "Two against two would be fair odds, I think," McCollum took him up, his own voice taking on a ring. "Do you care to explain that, Captain Baird?" He had turned to face his visitor, bony hands stuck into his belt so that just two fingers of each hand showed.

After that it was simple. Baird told the full story, explaining why a different version had been given out. "So I'm left with three chores," he concluded. "First, I've got to see that Mrs. Rexford gets to St. Louis safely. Second . . ."

"I want to meet the lady," McCollum interrupted. "She must be quite a person."

"She is. And you'll meet her, of course. Socially. We want to make it appear that she has little interest in any of this. Mrs. Haislip will certainly manage to pass on the story to somebody behind Confederate lines and we don't want Mrs. Rexford's true activities known. If they find out how much she knows—or how much they even suspect she knows—it won't be so easy to keep a finger on some of the moves they're trying to make. Also, Mrs. Rexford may be a bit safer if she doesn't appear so dangerous to them."

"I'll be discreet. She is a League member, you say?"

"Yes. So is Corporal Warner. My second and third responsibilities are with regard to Warner and his men. I want to get them back to Denver without anyone giving them trouble for having gone so far from the area where they had scout duty. And Warner has to be relieved of his technical responsibility for those southern women." .

McCollum managed a weary smile. "I think maybe I can handle part of that. Suppose I leave you to read the various dispatches that have been waiting here for you? While you do that, I'll look in on your friends—in a social sort of way—and see about arranging a couple of matters."

"Fine. And you can ease off on your patrols. I don't think anybody's going to make any attacks anywhere in the immediate future."

When suppertime rolled around, Baird discovered that Captain McCollum had been spending a busy afternoon. The officer had discovered that there was a badly worn thimble skein on Mrs. Rexford's wagon.

Since the post wheelwright was doing patrol duty and would not return to the fort immediately, there would have to be a delay of two or three days before the wagon could be moved.

Which was most unfortunate, McCollum lamented, since the other two ladies could head east without delay. Three trade wagons and some twenty mules had come up from Santa Fe with a variety of trade goods but had halted at Fort Larned because of the attack rumors. Now they could move again. Their leader held a New Mexico militia commission so it would be perfectly legal to give him the orders Warner had taken from another New Mexico militia officer.

"One of your problems settled," McCollum told Baird privately. "You get rid of those women. I hope you don't feel too badly that they will be traveling with a gang of mule skinners."

"Captain, you are a genius," Baird laughed. "I'll mention you in my report. No details, of course."

By that time he had worked out problem number two for himself. Using the letter Governor Gilpin had given him, he simply wrote a return note on the back of the paper:

This is to certify that Corporal Ethan Warner, Private Luis Martinez and Private Dirk Jaggers, the sole surviving members of a scout patrol of the First Colorado Cavalry, have performed outstanding service in cooperation with the undersigned as requested in the letter of Governor Gilpin. Their devotion to duty has resulted in renewed safety for the military posts and settlements along the Arkansas River. Because of the need for continued secrecy in some of these matters, no report in writing can be made. Corporal Warner can supply all necessary information.
(signed)
Thomas Baird, Captain U.S.A.

He handed the paper to Warner before going in to the supper McCollum was giving for the ladies. "You've got a lot of leeway there, Ethan," he said with a grin. "Tell him the truth and don't try to add any fancy stuff."

"Hell, Cap'n, he ain't even gonna believe the truth. But I'll give it a try."

Supper in the post commander's quarters became the same sort of wryly amusing routine that had marked the last stage of the journey. Mrs. Davenport was still mentally squirming. She knew perfectly well that something was being held back from her but she could not ask questions without betraying knowledge which she did not dare admit. Partly because of that feeling of frustration perhaps, she was the one who insisted on leaving early and getting back to the wagon.

When all of the polite exchanges had been made, there was finally a chance for Pat Rexford to stare quizzically at the two men and inquire, "How many fancy tricks were used around here today? This business of staying in the background has its drawbacks, I'm learning. I don't know what is going on."

"Lots of time to find out," Baird told her solemnly. "I got a lot of valuable information in the mail today. Things like warnings to look into a mysterious conspiracy supposedly called Cimarron Thunder and a memo not to bother with the Captain Madison rumor since he is known to be on the Mississippi now. Also a belated warning that the government agent I am supposed to meet is a woman and that I should conduct myself accordingly."

"I wonder what they mean by that," she murmured.

"Obvious, isn't it? A woman should be treated as a woman." He frowned heavily as he added, as though talking to himself, "That means I don't treat her as a gun-crew member—or a nurse—or a scout—or as a horse holder. This is going to take a lot of careful thought."

McCollum laughed aloud. "What a problem! Just

remember that you'll have to make a full report on everything you do."

"So do I," Pat told him. "This could get to be a problem."

"Like I just said," McCollum chuckled. "What a problem!"

Ride into the world of adventure with Ballantine's western novels!

Ballantine brings you the best of the West~ And the best western authors